Innocence

This Side of Innocence

BY RASHID AL-DAIF

TRANSLATED FROM ARABIC BY PAULA HAYDAR
WITH AN AFTERWORD BY ADNAN HAYDAR AND MICHAEL BEARD

Interlink Books
An imprint of Interlink Publishing Group, Inc.
New York • Northampton

First published in 2001 by

INTERLINK BOOKS
An imprint of Interlink Publishing Group, Inc.
99 Seventh Avenue • Brooklyn, New York 11215 and
46 Crosby Street • Northampton, Massachusetts 01060
www.interlinkbooks.com

Library of Congress Cataloging-in-Publication Data
Al-Daif, Rashid.
    [Nahiyat al-bara'a. English]
    This side of innocence / Rashid al-Daif ; translated from the Arabic
by Paula Haydar.
        p. cm. — (Emerging voices)
    ISBN 1-56656-383-6
    I. Haydar, Paula, 1965– II. Title. III. Series.
    PJ7820.A46 N3413 2001
    892.7'36—dc21   00-011236

Printed and bound in Canada

Cover painting "Beirut Today" (undated) by Suha Tamim, 1936–1986, courtesy of the Royal Society of Fine Arts, Amman, Jordan.

To request our complete 52-page full-color catalog,
please call us toll free at **1-800-238-LINK**, visit our
website at **www.interlinkbooks.com**, or write to
Interlink Publishing
46 Crosby Street, Northampton, MA 01060
e-mail: sales@interlinkbooks.com

Who tore the picture? That is the whole story, from A to Z. They wanted to know who tore the picture.

But be forewarned. I tell you now before I get started, and before I delve into the details, some of which might reveal a truth that is different from the one I'm trying to convey. I tell you now, with a clear conscience, that they did not mean me any harm, and this is very important. I'll also say I was not being targeted personally, and this, too, is of major importance.

They came in all of a sudden! Four men in civilian clothes. One sat down behind the desk, two others stood beside him, to his right, and a fourth stood to his left—he was the one who started questioning me.

They were men in every meaning of the word, and you could see their determination in every feature of their faces.

They weren't going to waste any time, nor were they going to allow any ambiguity or confusion to get in their way. If I had to summarize them in one word, I would say without hesitation: efficient! These were actual examples of what we hear a lot of talk about in our country, but rarely ever actually encounter.

They came in all of a sudden, walked over to the desk in conspicuous silence, and the moment they took their positions he began questioning me (the one I mentioned above). "Who tore the picture?"

The question put me at ease, really; it relieved my anxiety, because I understood from it what concerned me most of all—they didn't have anything against me personally. They only wanted my help in finding out who did it.

My relief was obvious. I noticed that they noticed it, and I also noticed they gave no indication my relief was out of place or inappropriate to the occasion.

But how quickly I also noticed that my feeling of ease, which must have been reflected in my facial expression, did not change their behavior in any way. They remained just as indifferent as before.

They possessed all the characteristics of real men, even if they were still just boys in terms of years.

When I began to answer, he interrupted me with renewed questioning. "I asked you who tore the picture!"

He repeated the question before I had uttered a single word. I had only begun to answer, so what was that supposed to mean? What did it mean for him to ask and not let me answer? Could he guess my answer before I even stated it? My face tightened again, and the wave of optimism that had come over me when he had asked the question earlier, declaring their good intentions toward me, dissipated. The way he interrupted me (I say it plainly) irritated me, because it threw me off. I mean, it surprised me. Why didn't he trust me? And why wouldn't he wait to hear my answer, which might contain the very thing he was looking for? Or did he feel that I wasn't going to give a good enough answer, so he raised his voice hoping to push me to give him more. But how? How could I give him more, when what he was after was the truth, and the truth was very thing I was going to give him and nothing less.

This was precisely the problem.

He wanted me to tell the truth, and all I wanted to tell was the truth and nothing but the truth. But how?

Yes! I admit truthfully that when they came in I was surprised! Yes! I admit that.

p of yes!

I was surprised, even though for some time I had been expecting them to come, one of them anyway, or someone at least. With that I had made my first mistake, the first in an unending series of them.

o Same

The moment they entered I stood up—and I didn't have to stand up—thereby making my second mistake. (And was I really not supposed to stand up?)

Then, even after they sat down, I kept standing—yes, standing—thus setting off a chain reaction of mistakes.

Here, before being completely taken with remembering the events of those critical hours, I must clarify the following matter: only now do I realize that those were mistakes; only now do I realize that those were precisely the mistakes that cost me what I can never make up for with what I still have left in terms of mental and physical well-being. (It's difficult for me to say, "What I still have left in terms of years.") And I say "only now" because during those critical moments I was incapable of deriving any meaning from my behavior, or seeing any purpose to it, or realizing what kind of effect it might have.

But I'm not saying all this just to mull over some grief I would be better off forgetting, but rather to give a warning and a lesson—and that's a matter no two people can argue over. The warning and the lesson are intended for me, certainly, but for other people, too, especially for other people, because what happened to me can never happen again. Such a thing can only happen to one person, one time. For it to happen again would make life itself impossible, and making life impossible is a very serious matter indeed.

Their faces were unambiguous.

And they shared a certain familiarity with each other.

But what bewildered me most of all was that they didn't ask me my name first, nor did they ask me later on. How could they not be interested in knowing the name of the person they were interrogating, the person from whose answers they expected to glean the truth? Were they, these men of great experience, ignorant of the usefulness of knowing names in such situations? The name might save them all their trouble. After all, doesn't the name determine everything else? I was waiting for the right moment to tell them my name, but they constantly prevented me from it. I couldn't figure out what secret lay behind this behavior, and what was the point.

"Open your mouth only when you're asked to!"

This is what I was bombarded with whenever I started to talk.

Why would an interrogator forbid the person under interrogation from revealing his name? This was something I simply could not figure out. So I thought that maybe there was some wisdom in it, and it would be smart to just go along with it. I backed off of my attempts to reveal my name then, which was definitely very painful. No, it was suffocating. But it wasn't the first time I had yielded to the dictates of a situation. So often a person is forced to "swallow" a difference of opinion, or a surprise reaction, or a misunderstanding, or even an insult sometimes.

4

And they didn't ask my age either! And I, with my age nearing a hefty sum, don't usually like to be asked about my age, but it does impose certain rules; it carries a kind of respectability. I wanted badly to tell them my age, but if they didn't allow me to tell them my name, why would they let me tell them my age?

"Open your mouth only when you're asked to!"

This was fired at me whenever I began to say anything that was against all logic not to say.

My face tightened, in an obvious way, but nothing about them changed. They remained indifferent; they were there, but absolutely unshakable.

And what really amazed me was that they never interrupted one another, or disagreed, or accused each other of making mistakes or anything like that.

So all this amazed me, but I tried using intellect and logic to comprehend my feeling of amazement, just as I had always tried before—since I had entered—to comprehend all of the emotions that came over me and imposed themselves upon me, the surprise when they came in, irritation when one of them interrupted me, suffocation when they forbade me from revealing my name and age, and so on. No doubt this constant battle of mine against all these emotions had a negative influence on my actions. And it influenced (in turn) the succession of events and the level they reached in the end.

And I say in all honesty that I am always wary of my emotions. They always lead me where I don't want to go. I always end up in situations that at the very least can be called emotionally-exhausting, problem-causing predicaments. For exactly this reason, I was careful from the moment I was brought in to the office, to be myself; that is, to be balanced,

5

cool, collected, to use my head and be enlightened by it. Actually, even more than that, I was careful from the start not to *appear* natural, but to *be* natural.

Be natural!

I understood deeply and sharply that the difference between the two conditions (appearing or being) is very significant, no matter how trivial it might seem to hasty, unthinking people.

These two good qualities, being natural and being mindful, were the first things I had to put to the test, starting the very moment I found myself in that place—the man leading me by the arm had opened the door to an office, pushed me inside, and shut the door, leaving me all alone.

"What about dignity?"

"What about dignity?" I almost shouted, loud enough for that crude and insufferable man to hear me through the door he had shut so fast, but I quickly sized up my situation (Stupidity is so ugly. Especially at such critical moments) and turned to my "self," spoke to my "self," called out to my "self" in a voice so clear and decisive it was nearly audible. I said, "Calm down, man!"

Then I repeated it with even more force, so that I could almost hear it, like a gunshot. "Calm down!"

"The ground is still beneath your feet, the sun is still shining in the sky, and the human race is the same as ever, making mistakes sometimes and getting things right sometimes... So calm down!"

As I shouted this to my self, I imagined my lips mouthing the words in silence.

Then, just a few moments after the onset of this determination of mine, everything within me began to yield to me and respond completely to my will.

6

Now, after I had the situation completely under control, I said, "I need to sit down." So I sat down.

There were several fancy leather couches in the office—three or four—I don't remember exactly how many any more. I sat on the one closest to the window, with my back to the window. Through a transparent white curtain that covered the window (the only one in the room) came a flood of light that lit up the whole room. I chose this particular spot on purpose, with the wisdom of experience, for I knew from things I had read and from social etiquette that a guest, if below his host in rank and importance, should sit in a spot where the light will shine directly on his face—in other words, the opposite of what I did—to make it easy for the latter to get a good look at him. Using this approach, I intended for my host to realize—subconsciously if not consciously—that he was not in the presence of some disregarded, useless nobody.

I chose this spot then, "*en connaissance de cause*," as they say in French.

And also, by choosing this spot, I wanted to prove to my self—yes, to my self—that it was not by furious, primal screaming (which is what it—my self, that is—wanted to do) that honor and dignity were protected, but rather by following a wise, intelligent, and appropriate course of action. If I had left it up to nature, I would have screamed, "What about dignity!"

Then the man who had pushed me into the room that way (totally inappropriately I say) would have come back at me and treated me even worse. He might have even crossed the line from stern words to insults. Or maybe he would have crossed the line completely from words to other things, ugly things, like beating me up for example, or kicking me all over uncontrollably, all over my body, in the shins, for example, or the knees, or the balls.

7

"Your tongue"—so say our Arab forbears—"is your horse. Mind it and it will mind you!"

Anger, even if it is the complete opposite of contentedness (and I certainly was not content), is reprehensible. Even if it is justified?

Yes, I say now, even if it is justified, anger is reprehensible. My painful ordeal has taught me that much. (Yes—it was an ordeal, and it was painful, and I describe it this way freely, frankly.)

For if the man had hit me or kicked me, he would merely have been exercising a right extended to him in accordance with the strict orders given him by his superiors. And even if I had shouted at him to treat me with some respect, and he didn't respond with the severity due me according to the law, then he would have put himself in the position of having shirked his responsibilities and would therefore deserve punishment. What if one of his ignorant, empty-headed superiors, completely unaware of what was going on, were to hear me shouting, and then see him just sit there and do nothing. What would he do?

So I sat down like any self-respecting, respectful person would do. After all, a couch in such a place, like any other seat, is meant for sitting on, as long as it's unoccupied.

So I sat down, then, exercising my rights as a person standing in a place full of empty seats. (At that time I didn't know that later on comfort would not come from sitting down.) I leaned back, crossed my legs, and waited, examining every corner and every object in the room.

I waited.

Unfortunately I didn't have a newspaper anymore. The man who led me to that place snatched it from my hand before I got

8 took his connection to outside

to the door. I don't know how he noticed it when he never really looked at me carefully after receiving me in that dark corridor from the two who had brought me into the building. He didn't search me, either, and neither did the two other men.

I didn't have a magazine or a book or anything to read. There was nothing of the sort anywhere.

Behind the desk there was an elegant wooden bookcase with fat books with fancy bindings on shelves protected behind locked glass doors. But the titles weren't showing. In fact, there wasn't a single letter or number showing on them at all. So what were they? Files, maybe? Secret files? Well if that was the case, I should forget about them; act as if they were not there. My eyes never fell upon them. (After all, what thing exists without its secrets? What institution, what country, what political party…what club? Right?)

Then I happened to look at my hand. And why wouldn't I, when I was looking all around the room, inspecting everything in it, one object at a time! And how can I blame myself this time for yielding to spontaneity? Is there anything more logical than for you to look, even without planning to, at your own hand, while waiting for whatever or whomever is coming?

I had a watch on my wrist. Well, who doesn't have one?

I do admit, though, it's not like other watches.

(I say honestly now, that is, during these moments while I convey what happened, that I'm not really sure this had any negative impact. At the same time I will also say, after long consideration, that I'm not at all sure it had a positive impact either. The presence of this watch on my wrist didn't change anything—I now believe—in the way the events unfolded, nor did it leave the slightest impression.)

The watch was made in Japan. Casio, Quartz, water-resistant.

A number was printed at the bottom edge of the frame: 901A2-T18, followed by the word JAPAN, then the letter N, in a curved line parallel with the watch's frame, which was round. The letters were so tiny I couldn't make them out with the naked eye, as though they were some kind of secret writing. But I was able to read them eventually, once I got out alive. (I say alive because it's the right word. What happened, even though it might not have been the responsibility of anyone present there, almost got me killed.) So I was saying then that I read the letters after getting out alive, with the aid of a magnifying glass. I breathed in deeply after reading them, filling my lungs with air. I had a strange desire to suck in a lot of air, which was because I didn't find anything about the tiny writing on the edge of the watch that was cause for alarm. So why had I been afraid that the interrogators would be alarmed if they happened to see it, or find it suspicious, even if they were to assume the worst.

(Is it wrong to call them interrogators?)

I looked over that watch as I hadn't looked over it since buying it roughly two years earlier, as I had never looked over it ever before. Indeed, maybe as I had never looked over anything before. It was the only "gadget" (if you like) I was carrying at the time.

Then I noticed, while I was still looking over the watch, that a lot of time had passed, maybe half an hour—I don't remember now—in which I had sat all alone, waiting, though no one opened the door.

There on the desk, to the side closest to where I was sitting, was a telephone, right near me, within reach. I tried hard to guess if it worked or not, but how could I guess without lifting the receiver up to my ear; and I didn't do that, nor do I regret it one bit.

Half an hour passed and I was still sitting in the same position. I took off my watch, though, and turned it over, examining it from every angle. On the metal back was the following innocent information:

CASIO

371 Mo-82

STAINLESS STEEL BACK

WATER RESISTANT

JAPAN C

I say innocent information, and I mean by that the common type of information we see everyday. No, every minute, on everything we bump into, everywhere we go, always written in Latin script, with numbers and names of far away countries, and strange brand names and odd markings. So what was there to be suspicious about then? Unless…unless these things, or some of them anyway, were really codes that only the people they were intended for can understand, codes used to send secrets the rest of us are completely unaware of. But…but even so, I can still state, innocently, that they are innocent, in the sense that they are so widely circulated and as common as the air we breathe, and in the sense that their secrets don't involve us.

I didn't have a newspaper or a magazine or a book or anything to read, so all I could do was wait. (Plain wait.)

There was a big, fancy rug in the room covering a big section of the floor, which was carpeted wall to wall.

A bookcase, a desk, couches, a carpet with a rug on top, painted walls! This was a room for people of "*classe*," no doubt about it, and such people had no reason to harm anybody. I had no need to worry.

Everything in the room was clean, too, very clean. Luckily, the clothes I was wearing were clean, so I had nothing to be ashamed of. I had taken a shower that morning before leaving the house, and changed into a nice clean pair of white underwear. The one thing, though, that might cause me some embarrassment, was that I had walked pretty far before ending up there in that office, and my legs always sweat so much…But these were just negative thoughts coming to me, which stemmed from the nature of the situation I had unexpectedly found myself in. Anyway, if matters were to get any worse, I was going to have to face quite a bit of embarrassment. I am very shy, for example, about showing my body to strangers, male or female, so how could I possibly show it there? (I thought that if anything was going to happen it was going to happen right there.) I, who never goes to the beach or swimming pools because of this shyness, and who, even on intimate occasions, always turns off the lights or dims them at least.

But these were surely just negative thoughts.

Ever since I was very young I never showed anyone, no matter how close they were to me, anything private. Even when I needed a doctor, I would manage to outsmart him into not making me get undressed. So how on earth could I dare do it now (even if forced to) at this age, and in front of a bunch of youngsters who now had my fate in their hands.

And you know, younger types of interrogators, in these situations, demand so much from the person they're interrogating. So much. For example, they demand he doesn't leave one scrap of clothing to cover his nakedness. Yes! Even underwear!

Then they make him turn around.

And then, as soon as he turns around, one of them comes closer, from behind—gets very close! Meanwhile the others come from the front, so if he tries to escape they can beat him up.

And if he can't get an automatic erection, they poke him with needles.

(Not medically sound? Maybe.)

But as I said before, all of this was just hallucinations and negative thoughts that were coming to me as a natural result of the tension that was building in that hour of waiting.

So an hour went by while I waited for someone to come in and ask me a question, or if possible, I would try to get an explanation out of him. But no one came. There wasn't even the hint of a sound, or an echo, or any sign of anyone, human or otherwise. All I could hear, with alarming clarity, was the rustle of my clothes whenever I moved against the leather of the couch I was sitting on.

That place could not but seem very strange to the unknowing, carefree person, that place, which was totally impervious to all of the clamor of the city. No car, no horn, no motorcycle, nothing whatsoever, even though it was right in it—in this very city—right in the heart of it, on one of its main streets clamoring with cars and pedestrians, and right in the middle of the day. (I knew exactly which building I was in.)

All the while I just sat, for an hour and a half, not moving at all except to lift one leg off another, or cross one leg over another, and even that I didn't overdo!

And you know, it's not easy for a person to sit all that time, with nothing to keep busy with, like a newspaper for example, or a book, or a TV screen, or conversation, or anything else. And not just sit, either, sit and wait. And what a wait!

I'm not saying all this just to grumble or complain or describe some hardship I suffered, but to give an idea of the atmosphere I was in—the pressure—which facilitated my doing what I did, and which prevented me from predicting what the results of the steps I was taking would be, or the potential dangers. In short, in just that atmosphere, I made the other mistake—the big mistake—the one no man can forgive of another man and which, if I were to forgive myself for it, I could never forget. And that is, from the time I entered that room, I had succeeded in resisting my desire to smoke—with a full pack of cigarettes in my pocket. My intention in refraining from smoking was to kill two birds with one stone: first, smoking is bad for you, according to current popular wisdom. I should quit sooner or later, and here was an opportunity to start, or at least get used to the idea; and second, the room was closed up, no open windows or any I could see anyway, and smoking in there would choke anyone who came in—and there's the point of the story: the breath of anyone who entered would be choked off, and that would make him extremely angry, and rightly so! As if he had been belted in the stomach unawares. The situation was bordering on life-or-death.

Over and above all these aforementioned reasons, there were other reasons that were no less significant, no matter how they seemed at first: the days when smoking was fashionable were long over. Today smokers are like the sick, who need special care, which is exactly what I had always taken great pains not to appear to be: weak-willed, led by my impulses rather than in control of them. That was exactly what would lessen the amount of respect people I met would have for me—if not wipe it out altogether—when my whole life depended on it—this respect—since without it, I would find myself in a condition of misery few people would begrudge me.

For two hours I fought my craving, which kept goading me more and more to smoke.

For two hours I fiddled with my watch, playing with it like worry beads.

Then suddenly, like an electric shock, my mind was charged with the fact that the numerals on my watch were in Arabic!

Yes, in Arabic! Unlike all the watches everyone else in the world wears on their wrists.

All the watches belonging to all the Arabs in the whole, entire universe had foreign numerals except for mine.

It was not as if I was completely unaware of this fact, because I was the one who chose that watch and no other watch. I was the one who bought that watch and no other watch. See, when I saw it on display, it caught my attention. It seemed "*originale*" and it was pretty cheap. I needed a watch, so I bought it. After a while I just got used to it and didn't think of it as being so special anymore. The same happened among my friends and buddies; it no longer caught their attention, or aroused any conversation. But let's be honest, it set them wondering quite a bit at first. They pestered me a lot with their questions—and they were all friends and buddies, some of the closest people to me in the world! They wanted me to spell out the real reason I had bought it. Yes, the real reason. What a nuisance that was: my friends pestering me about the real reason I had bought that watch. My answer didn't satisfy them, which was, in all simplicity, that I thought it was a novelty, and it was cheaper than all the other watches on display, which were much like the ones they themselves were wearing. Yes, I remember now, unfortunately, that one of them asked me—even if he was joking—if the real reason wasn't to be found in my "Arab nationalist sentiments." I set about answering him, with a smile no less, despite all the laughter and surprise at his brilliant observation, saying that such sentiments were nowhere in my mind when I bought the watch. He asked if it might have been a subconscious impulse then, so I said I couldn't be certain about that one way or the other.

Then my friends forgot about the numerals on my watch and grew accustomed to it, except... except sometimes, over long intervals.

Then, the truth be told, no one close to me or otherwise would see it for the first time without it catching their attention. Some showed this outright, while others went further than that and asked about it, and others asked questions that already contained the answer—I mean the Arab nationalism reasons. In fact, once someone proclaimed in his question that behind my purchase was a kind of nationalistic fanaticism.

It wasn't easy for me to get over my shock at having noticed the numerals on my watch, because the result of stirring up the subject with the interrogators could turn out to be very dangerous, and not because they themselves might not possess this Arab nationalist sentiment, which every genuine Arab possesses, but rather because this sentiment was simultaneously an instrument of unification and division.

But I had to get over the shock so the situation would not get completely out of hand. I continued fiddling with the watch, trying to forget, until I noticed that the word JAPAN was marked three times in three different places. The first one was at the bottom of the face, the second on the back of the watch, and the third on the inside of the wristband. I told myself that this little observation was hardly worth pause, but despite my judgment against its significance, I felt it must have originated from some great, deep source. I thought that the word JAPAN three times on this small object was a bit much, too much, unnatural! *TROP! C'EST TROP!*

Time continued to advance, and I continued to sit, moving only to lower one leg off the other, or cross one leg over the other. My economy of movement was based on a clear and carefully thought out plan: I wanted their impression of me when they came in to be positive. Their first impression was very important. If, at first sight, they saw me fidgeting a lot, then maybe they would think I was nervous. And then they might wonder why, make all kinds of assumptions, and treat me accordingly. Moreover, remaining seated showed composure, poise, and good upbringing, too.

I noticed, suddenly, even as I waited, that I was there, waiting. It was very strange how I always noticed things all of a sudden, even if I was noticing things once every second. And that's how the situation remained up until the incredible transformation occurred—I mean with the light.

The light changed.

The light changed dramatically while I was wrapped up in all the writings and numerals. As if all of a sudden.

It was as if the sun had suddenly gone down behind some building that blocked its light. With this momentous change, it occurred to me that all the things I had been thinking about previously were mere trivialities. Now I had to face reality head-on, and quit wasting time on all that nonsense I was passing the time with, such as contemplating the watch, for example, and even sillier things, like contemplating the shoes I spent so much time examining, and which attracted my attention quite a bit. In fact I say unequivocally: it really bothered me that the soles of my shoes were made of thick AIR GUM with an air pocket in the end of the heel that was a different color than the rest of the sole, which made it stand out quickly and easily from the right or the left. That was the only interesting thing about the shoes. The rest was not very special. There was one other distinguishing characteristic, though—if it's all right to call it that—not about the shoes themselves, but rather about the way I got them. I didn't buy them myself. They came as a present from overseas, but not from any foreigners, from a friend of mine living overseas. Business purposes, that's all, not thoughtfulness or anything else. No cause for suspicion. Really, I'm ready and willing right now to declare, before anyone gets the wrong idea, using everything I know about the matter, without any shame or hesitation, especially since—and this is what I must never forget, even in the event that none of them mentions it— especially since the person who carried them from overseas for me was not a friend of mine, nor a friend of my friend's, but a friend of a friend of my friend. What's more, I wasn't even home when he brought them (so where was I then?). The owner of the store in my building received them from him. I never saw him.

I never saw the man, or the woman, or the person, rather, and I never found out his name, or his age for that matter, or anything else about him. As far as I'm concerned, he never existed. But wait...

Wait! I did find out something about him. I mean, about her. Now it's all coming back to me. When the storeowner gave me the shoes I asked him who delivered them, and he said it was a woman. I asked him a lot about her. He said she was in her thirties, darkish coloring, medium height, pretty face—he said, smiling—and nice figure, too—he nearly laughed. He also said she asked him if he was likely to see me and could she leave this package with him, which had a pair of shoes inside it, because she hadn't found me at home. He answered her warmly, "Yes, of course!" He said it and smiled again.

I don't know what kept making me think I had been arrested for some serious crime, or as if any minute I would be subjected to a sharp interrogation by an expert interrogator and bully. I don't know what the cause for such excessive pessimism was, considering that everything that was happening called for facing things head on with confidence and optimism, not this delving into unfounded negative thoughts that were sure to keep cropping up when examined carefully through the lens of pure, rational thinking.

It was getting very late. Very, very late. A lot more than two hours had gone by, maybe even—who knows—more than three hours. I couldn't judge the time at all anymore, because with all that fiddling with the watch and playing with it like worry beads of course I had messed with the spring pin and moved the hands ahead (or back), and now there was no way to determine the correct time and fix it, because when I had done it, I hadn't realized I had done it. It didn't even cross my mind until the light changed the way it did so dreadfully, and so suddenly.

time stops due to his action

First I thought I must have inadvertently nodded off and the sun set while I was dozing. What made me think so was that from time to time I had felt sleepy waiting there on that couch for so long, although I wouldn't allow myself to fall asleep. In such a situation that would show an enormous lack of respect.

So I figured I must have dozed off for a while without realizing it. But then in a moment of awareness I became certain that I never closed my eyes for a second. I was sure of that. Further, this sleepiness I had felt wasn't actually sleepiness, but in fact just a kind of stupor I was in from sitting still for so long.

True, the room was very quiet, and that encouraged a feeling of ease, but the anxiety that was deepening little by little, and which I was succeeding to resist, undoubtedly prevented me from being careless and falling asleep.

Then suddenly I found myself getting up off the couch, standing on my feet, ready to make that other mistake I can't even describe. But this particular mistake, in the final analysis and after careful consideration, was not in standing up exactly, but in the sudden way I stood up, as if it happened on its own, with no prior decision from me. And this, despite the fact that I had trained myself, little by little over the course of my stay there, not to give myself any surprises, to make sure any movement I made was the result of a conscious, calculated decision, a premeditated decision, with careful attention having been given to all its details, intricacies, stages, and most of all, its proper moment of action. I had succeeded in nearly everything up until the moment I stood up. Not only had I not smoked, I hadn't even taken the pack of cigarettes out of my pocket, the way I usually do when I'm trying not to smoke, so if anyone suddenly came in they wouldn't catch me holding it. That successful decision was based on reasons I had already studied very carefully and thought through completely. You see, it occurred to me that the cigarettes I had were American. Marlboros, which are the most popular brand in Lebanon. (By popular I mean the most consumed.) If someone came in all of a sudden and saw them in my hand it would lead him to lump me in with everyone else, to consider me one of the immeasurable masses, one among the infinite many, a grain of sand on a seacoast or in a desert, indistinguishable from all the rest except under careful scrutiny. And that was what would lead the intruder, without the slightest doubt, to treat me accordingly—like some disregarded creature wandering aimlessly about. (It never crossed my mind before that cigarettes categorized people to such a degree—it's amazing how ideas come to a person if he wants to think. How they come if he wants them to!) So I had decided that taking the pack of cigarettes out of my pocket and holding it in my hand would not be in my best interest, and I acted in careful accordance with this decision. And the same went for the lighter, for more than what the cigarette pack contained the lighter contained fire.

Yes, the lighter contained fire!

But the point was that suddenly and spontaneously I stood up. After that, it didn't mean anything that I could sit back down if I wanted to before anyone barged in on me. It didn't mean anything that my spontaneous, unplanned standing up did not pose any direct threat to me. The danger had been in the act of making the mistake, not in the mistake itself or its consequences.

But, in spite of everything, this standing up out of the fear that suddenly overcame me (let's call things by their names) when the light changed, was the basic turning point in the succession of events that began the moment I had been brought to that place. Then, after the period of hesitation that did not last very long, I said: now that the mistake has been made, let me learn something from it. (Strange how things develop sometimes, in directions we would never predict, without us having any hand in them.) I took a step, but not in any particular direction. (I was totally conscious of that.) Then another step, and a third, the goal being to move around a bit and shake off the pain of having sat still for so long. Then I stretched, and turned around to face the window and look at it a long time, hoping to see what was behind the white curtain.

But I couldn't make anything out, which was strange since it was a white curtain and transparent, and the amount of light coming through it was more than enough to be able to see everything inside the room clearly, despite the change in it that had terrified me. So what was beyond the window, then?

Fear is reprehensible, no matter what the reasons or causes. It is reprehensible and unacceptable, because it simply stops the brain from functioning, and all objective, scientific thought becomes paralyzed, allowing irreparable damage to be done, and that, fortunately, was exactly what came quickly and clearly into my mind, and what served as the basis of my subsequent actions.

What was beyond the window?

Now I was faced with a well-defined problem (which had presented itself, too, with no input from me). And that transformed my situation. I shifted to a new state, different from the one I had been in before in which I forged ahead (in my mind) aimlessly.

The motivation behind this goal I now found myself aiming toward was not to know the unknown, or uncover the hidden, or reveal the secret. No, it was not that at all. Nor was I planning to escape, and I definitely was not preparing a surprise of any kind. It was nothing but simple, natural, curiosity. It is elementary for a person to want to know the place he or she is in, with no intentions of taking any action of any kind.

Accordingly, I made the decision.

It was a clear decision. I would only advance as far as the window and then look through it, but only in order to find out what was outside. And this very simple decision, with respect to physical exertion anyway, and with respect to the small investment in time it required as well, called for an incredible amount of both daring and caution. It was important, first of all, in order to reach the window that I go around the couch, which would mean crossing a distance of roughly two meters, thereby exposing myself to possible surprise by a sudden intruder. In such a suspicious position—it would be quite natural for such an intruder to wonder what I was up to; it wouldn't look like the kind of behavior one would expect from someone waiting to be interrogated about a serious crime—I would thereby be exposing myself to a lot of suspicion (and serious suspicion this time) right when what I needed most was to cast off suspicion, and cast off anything that would give them reason to base their suspicions on proof (especially palpable proof) and to use this suspicion to justify arresting me as a perpetrator caught in the act. Let's suppose, for example, that I made it around the couch and got within a few steps of the window, advancing with the necessary amount of caution, and someone entered and then asked me (after surely getting a bit shaken up—the consequence to be very serious for me for sure—because he wasn't expecting to find the person he was coming to interrogate in this position), and asked me, "What are you doing there?" What would I answer? What would I say? Would I, for example, be able to explain myself? Or would I have put myself in a very compromising position, a grave position rather. I, who had decided from the very start to make truth my leader, my quest, my one desire! Why then should I do what was prohibited? Why even approach the forbidden things? And what kind of fool would believe it was just curiosity? And was it really just curiosity? Further, if I had lied to myself and believed the lie, was I capable of lying to others and deceiving them into believing me, too? (And what others they were!)

23

Despite all this, I proceeded toward the window, considering
every possibility and how to confront each one, basing
everything on my deep-seated conviction that I was innocent
of everything that had gotten me into that place. I say
innocent, but it's more appropriate to say "at peace with
myself," because the word "innocent" might bring up, by
negative association, the word "guilty."

The decision to proceed, therefore, was very sensitive and
critical, and going through with it required, as I already
mentioned before, an amount of moral courage I don't believe
is available to just anyone, especially if we consider that I did
have the other, obvious option, which was to go back to sitting
on the couch and staying there without moving until
something I had nothing to do with happened, like someone
coming in on me or something like that. That solution was
very tempting for its simplicity and especially for its lack of
risk. Indeed, not choosing it was a very bold step. (All courage
is relative.)

When I reached the curtain I didn't touch it. I just stood in
front of it and looked through, trying to get a glimpse of
something outside, and being careful at the same time not to
touch it or let any part of my body or clothing touch it
either—because no matter what, I was responsible. This
caution with the curtain wasn't out of special concern for the
curtain itself, as if it were a trap or something, or was hiding
some trap, or as if it had been put there for some purpose other
than the one it had been created for. No, my caution was
merely part and parcel of the general caution I had taken as a
basic principle for all my actions in that room, from the
moment I was brought there. Actually, it is a principle I always
adhere to in life in general, a foundation upon which I base my

dealings with people's possessions and things. I've always believed there's a lot of respect in that for them as people; it's their right and my duty. It's a way, which I've always considered the best way, of making other people treat me with the kind of respect I want to be treated with.

I couldn't make out anything outside, as though that curtain preceded a block of light instead of a window. As if this block of light, which was the same dimensions as the window, had been secured into the wall behind the curtain in place of the window, its exact same size, length, width, and depth.

More importantly, it was impossible to see through it. It was white as a block of ice. So where was the light coming from, then? Was it electric light, not coming in through the window from outside? Had I been unaware of this all that time? I closed my eyes and tried really hard to recall how the light was when I was first brought into the room. Was it sunlight or electric light? Were there distinct shadows, or were they suppressed under well-tested, artificial lighting? Where was I? I mean, what kind of place was I in? Was it just a regular room in a house set up as a study, or was it a business office, or what? It was more like— compared with rooms and offices I had seen before—a lawyer's office. (I smiled when this idea came to mind.)

Strange!

So where in the world was I then? I mean, what kind of place had I been put in? What was it called? Was it above ground or underground? How deep underground? Did it receive fresh air and sunlight? Did it...? Was it...? All these questions rained down on me, each one in itself capable of tearing down a mountain, so you can imagine what all of them together were like.

"Don't think like that, man! Pull yourself together! Act like a normal person, a respectable person. All of this is just a bad experience that will pass. A misunderstanding that will be cleared up. As soon as everything is laid on the table, you'll be out in the spring sunshine, headed wherever you like. Be strong."

That was right. I should not surrender. I should be strong, especially now that it was clear and specific what I was up against. It was also very important to me, regardless of the circumstances that had brought me there, to know where I was. And it was important to know what happened to the light, and how it had been when I first entered, and if it really had changed, and where was it coming from now? Indeed, all those questions challenged my intelligence, or rather my self-confidence. Could it have been possible that so much had happened without my being aware of any of it, as if I were some cat in a bag? If there was an excuse for not being aware of many things since I had gotten there, there was no excuse for not being aware of the light. What had been its nature? And what had it transformed into? And how? When I entered, it had been bright, clear, delightful. Yes, I had been delighted. I don't forget that for a second, because it had been the sign—from the first second—that I was innocent. What was going on was a mere misunderstanding. A mistake quickly to be fixed. Certainly a guilty man would not be put in a place that radiated with such light and clarity. (I don't say this to be truthful, necessarily, but to state the reality of the situation.) I would even go so far as to say that being put there would alleviate some of the guilt whoever gave the order to pick me up (arrest me) might be feeling, or at least it would alleviate his feeling of uncertainty. That in itself was something very positive. So then how did the light change? What happened, and did it really change? Was it not in my capacity to remember if sunlight or some other kind of light had cast the shadows, like electric light, for example? And is there any kind of light besides these two?

There I was, still standing there contemplating whatever that thing the curtain preceded was, which was supposed to be a window but wasn't a window, all the while my urgent desire to know what was going on around me giving rise to all these ideas. Innumerable ideas came to my mind. Some good, and some not so good. Some bad, and one really superb idea. No, brilliant, to the effect that I had to differentiate between my desire to know where I was and what kind of place it was on the one hand, and the nature of my being there and wanting to get out of there on the other. That would help me to dedicate myself to exclusively technical matters having nothing to do with feelings and emotions like fear, terror, constraint, impatience, and so on. This would set me straight, give me a firm grip on matters, and put me in charge. If I were absorbed in trying to know the room's location in the building, for example, I would forget I was waiting. Same thing if I tried to figure out the puzzle of the nature of the light, I would forget about the imminent investigation. Thus, getting absorbed in technical details would make me forget my anxiety, and I would thereby conquer it.

That idea was a great success and it had a very positive effect. It distanced me from those negative thoughts that had begun to sweep me away and cause me to begin to lose control of myself—a situation which, had it happened, would have been the end of me. Indeed, it would have been the end of them, too, because it would have dragged them into making a mistake, and I would be responsible.

Then, all of a sudden, the lights went out!

The lights went out. The room was draped in total darkness. I have never claimed to be courageous, nor did I ever want to be, but I did keep control of myself. I mean I got a good hold on myself and kept standing right where I was. I didn't get all excited (I mean I didn't become so unsettled as to go into a state of panic), and I didn't make any move I would come to regret later on. Truly, I behaved with a nobility and heroism rarely seen.

It was dark, suddenly. I couldn't tell if my eyes were open or shut. In my pocket I had a lighter and a pack of cigarettes. First I took out the cigarettes, pulled one out, and then I took the lighter and lit the cigarette with it. I took a long drag while still holding the lit lighter in my hand, using it to look around the room. I saw only the same things I'd seen before, but now they appeared gloomier.

I kept the lighter lit long enough to be able to get around to the front of the couch and sit down. Then after I settled into it, and reassured myself I was physically and emotionally safe, I put out the lighter and left the burning cigarette the only glowing thing amidst that cruel darkness.

Then I crossed one leg over the other.

But I purposely did not allow myself to get carried away wondering about the nature of what was going on. In fact I decided with sharp consciousness to contemplate nothing but the cigarette ember. After all, why be alarmed and lose control? What was the use of that, especially since a mistake now would be fatal. For, if I were to leave things up to nature, I would be as unsettled as a fish out of water, or a chicken with its head cut off. I would turn the room upside down. I might break things, or smash them to pieces. Or I might break some part of me, some part of my own body. No one can know how things might progress when the hour is filled with the chaos that precedes death. (Did I say death? Oh vile tongue!) So I said, listen, man, you have to prevent all these mistakes from happening, because if they do happen, there will be no room for regret.

"Concentrate on the glowing cigarette. Concentrate only on it!"

I focused my eyes on it. I let it consume me completely, constantly, and I discovered that the ember breathed incessantly, as if it had lungs. I also discovered that something inside it erupted every once in a while. I could hear it and see it flame up. Then I discovered what really amazed me about it. It was truly a world of its own, caught up in its own happenings with no concern for us. And despite its apparent smallness, it was an immense and incredible world, inasmuch as it seemed, after taking a long, careful look at it, like a continent of fire, an entire universe, on the tip of a humble little cigarette. And really, sometimes the room was not big enough for that universe, which emanated so strongly in all directions that it nearly pushed back the walls. Other times it would die down and go back to being merely a small burning ember.

But happy moments don't last long.

Where was I going to flick the ashes? My imagination was swimming in delight over the amazing world of the glowing ember when I was alerted to this problem. My cigarette had burned about halfway down, I believe, but was there an ashtray in the room? Just as not too long before I had tried to remember how the light and the shadows had been when I was brought into the room, I now tried to remember if I had seen an ashtray back when I was passing the time inspecting all the contents of the room. I didn't remember a thing. This was the second time I had tried to remember something and didn't succeed. If I was not to blame for not having paid attention to the nature of the light at first, because I hadn't been in the right frame of mind for that—I, the carefree innocent—without a doubt I was to blame for not noticing the presence—or lack of presence—of an ashtray, because I was a smoker who could not go without smoking for very long, and ever since hiding cigarettes and not offering them to guests had become the new fashion I never entered any place without first making sure if there was an ashtray or not. In fact, the ashtray had become for me a way to gauge people's social class and their level, type, and system of education. I could tell if it was mixed, or strictly Arab, or American-based, or French, all by the cigarettes. So how could I have failed to notice this time? How strange! But why strange? And what's more, why blame myself? Why this pleasure in self-degradation? After all, I had been brought to this place not as a guest but quickly and nervously. What was feasible for a guest was not feasible for me in terms of taking time and wavering, picking and choosing. So the situation being as I've described, why blame myself in this unsubstantiated way? If it was natural for me to blame myself for a mistake I had actually made, it didn't necessarily follow that I should blame myself for getting unintentionally tangled up in a matter with which I had nothing to do.

The cigarette ash was getting very long. I cupped my hand under it so it wouldn't fall onto the floor, but maybe it had already fallen, and… the floor was carpeted. I lowered my leg from on top of the other one, and rubbed the carpet with that foot so that if it really had fallen, the ashes would blend into the carpet fibers and disappear. Then no one would notice even if they had suspicions. But the cigarette was still going; the ember still burned on its tip. The ashes were bound to fall again, or maybe even a third or fourth time, and then the burden would quickly be upon me to put it out. The problem of finding an ashtray or some alternative solution still remained. I got up from the couch and lit the lighter, keeping it away from my face, and ventured around the room with my eyes. I didn't find anything, so I let the lighter go out and shut my eyes, thinking up another approach. Then I lit the lighter again and moved forward, trying to get a closer look at things, but still didn't find anything. At this point, and to my dismay, there was no way to avoid bumping into the leg of the low table that had been placed right in the middle of the room. It made a loud noise and I would have fallen down if I hadn't regained my balance quickly. Unfortunately, however, the noise had already been made. I expected someone to come in to find out what was going on. Such a noise must be cause for concern; it might mean an attempt to escape, or maybe some kind of rebellion against not being able to escape (and why not? They had the right to think so), or something along those lines, something that might come to mind. Or maybe I was trying to remind them that I was still there, for example.

When I bumped into the table and almost fell down, I accidentally let the lighter go out. There I stood in the dark, in the middle of the room, waiting, not knowing which direction I was facing—toward the door, or the window, or a corner, or the wall. It pained me that someone might come in by surprise while I was in that confused and humiliating state. I got really, really mad, and out of sheer anger my eyes nearly welled up with tears. I nearly started to cry. I nearly burst into tears. I imagined my face in that forlorn darkness, tightening up and stretching out, contorting into subsequent random movement

31

outside all normalcy. It scared me. (A person's face really is very scary when he or she bursts into tears.) My face, now completely detached from me, scared me, and it pained me more to think that someone might see it in that strange, animal-like form. I thought it had been lucky for me that the lighter went out. But unfortunately, whoever might enter would immediately turn the lights on. For surely he would know the place well. My anger doubled and I really did begin to cry. I heard the first burst start to come, but with what strength I still had left, I told myself I would not lose my human dignity, and with a will that came I don't know from where, right at the brink of destruction, I managed to bring my total, catastrophic collapse to a screeching halt, and that when it was still only in its beginning stages. What helped me in that, and I don't deny it, were the few seconds that passed without anyone coming in, the longer period of time that followed, and then the fact that no one came in at all. I say now, with all honesty and pride, that it was a brutal moment (… and oh, how pleasing is the point in time which turns such harsh experiences into memories we talk about with pride and joy.) After that I began to regain control of everything—my situation, my self, my body. My whole body. My eyes yielded to me. My face returned to its usual shape. I almost even smiled. Maybe I did smile, for having gotten out of that disastrous mess safely. But unfortunately, the cigarette in my hand was still going, and the burning ember was still breathing strong, which meant I had to find a solution—and fast. So I shut my eyes this time, too, in that darkness no less, and thought of another approach. I lit the lighter again and quickly surveyed the floor, hoping that maybe I would find a bare spot where I could put out my cigarette, but the carpeting covered the entire floor. Not a single spot was left bare, not even in the farthest corners. So what was the solution? I had to figure it out quickly. Then suddenly, like a flash of inspiration, which came to me from I don't know where, I thought, why not stand the cigarette up on the desk and let it go out slowly on its own? Then afterwards I could just put it in my pocket. It was an especially good plan because the desk was covered with a pane of glass, so there was no danger the cigarette would leave any marks, or that it could start a fire anywhere, because there wasn't any breeze in the room that could make it fly up onto anything flammable. I went slowly over to the desk, by the light of the lighter, stood the burning cigarette butt on it, and sat down on the couch to rest from this unrivaled exhausting experience, from which I was still in the process of recovering, and watch the burning ash die down on the tip of the cigarette butt.

But the ember, even though it shrank a little, just kept breathing.

Then it kept breathing some more, in a suspicious way, constantly, resolutely, as if it were somehow outside the laws of fire on the tips of cigarette butts. It reached halfway down the cigarette butt. It got halfway down and still it breathed, dimming, and then flaring up with a persistent determination, outside everything having to do with logic and intelligence, until it crossed over the halfway point with astonishing determination. Then while I was completely and passionately attentive to the ember I noticed that I, too, was still breathing. I was panting faster and faster, as if I had suddenly run into a sniper zone. Then the ember's breathing began (finally!) to slow down, and its size became perceptibly smaller. Then it entered the final phase of going out, during which it remained for a long time so small you could barely see it. And then it went out.

At that point I closed my eyes, but I kept seeing it burning. After that I realized I had been inexcusably stupid. I had put the cigarette butt on the desk because it had a glass cover, because glass doesn't burn. So why had I been struck with what struck me? Why had I caught the ember's breathing affliction? But at least I had stopped panting before making this analysis, which in fact had nothing to do at all with fact, for I didn't catch the ember's breathing affliction out of fear of fire, but out of fear.

Plain fear.

Plain fear because something out of the ordinary perhaps was happening before me that I couldn't connect with anything stored in my brain. There was nothing like it. I had nothing to measure it against.

Really, a person must be very careful, even of his own self. I am saying this because I had a definite tendency to be fearful and cautious of everything in that office, and fearful for everything in it, too, especially of breaking something and being blamed for it and held accountable when the time for blaming and settling accounts came around. Indeed, I had become obsessed, and that was totally unacceptable.

After I rested up a bit, and the vision of the ember faded from my eyes, and I took in a deep breath and saw the humor in my thinking that catching the ember's breathing affliction was related to my fear of burning the office, I wanted another cigarette. I realized that the pack had fallen out of my hand when my leg bumped into the table and I almost fell. I wasn't at all worried, because I was sure I would find it, no problem, with a mere flick of the lighter and a glance down at the floor right by the table. And my prediction was correct. No sooner did I light the lighter than I saw the pack there between the table and the couch I had been sitting on. It is so true that a person's morale wields great influence over his success or failure. If he always expects the worst, the worst is surely what he'll get. But if he's an optimist, he can be sure that this optimism will reflect on him and a little of it at least will rub off on him. I grabbed the pack of cigarettes (all I had to do was bend over) and pulled out a cigarette. I lit it and calmly began to smoke it, enjoying it, delighting in it. And during that moment of delight I felt not that I had to pee, but rather that if I were to go to the bathroom right then, I could pee.

People concerned about health these days often advise drinking water, and that makes you have to use the bathroom. Even though generally speaking I don't always heed health advice, I do believe what is said about the importance of water, so I drink, especially in the morning when I get up. Before anything else I drink a glass, sometimes more, and then rather than having coffee with breakfast, I drink tea.

But I was not concerned about this feeling one bit, nor did I see myself as being in a situation like that of people who find themselves confined in some place, for some reason or another, and are forced to hold it for a very long time, longer than they have the strength to bear (and some of them say that if they lose control of themselves and urinate against their will, and if it were to happen in a particular place, then they would be forced to drink their urine and wash their faces with it.) As for me, I forgot the matter entirely. I forgot it immediately. Didn't think about it anymore. In fact, and contrary to what many people might imagine, I was in good spirits for having used the occasion as an opportunity to think the room must surely have a small bathroom. That was completely logical, especially since it was apparently used as an office, or at least a place of business.

I told myself that as soon as the electricity came back on (and certainly the electricity would come back on) I would find out for certain, and that would be easy because if there were a bathroom, the door would have to be inside the room somewhere, in order not to have to go outside the room to get to it. After all, the room seemed to be completely independent, not part of an apartment, or an office, or anything else. Therefore, its bathroom would be inside, unless it was shared, meaning out in the hallway, the possibility of which I completely disregarded due to the obviously high quality of the place.

So the matter of urinating did not worry me. On the contrary, thinking about it had been useful, because it made me think about the bathroom and alerted me to look for it, especially because it would also solve the problem of the ashtray, with respect to the cigarette butt situation.

Another factor that I haven't mentioned yet played a positive role in my lack of worry, too, which was that "holding it" was a problem that might worry some people who were advanced in years, but that was not the case for me—even if we're all headed in that direction!

No! No! I had to forget about it.

Indeed I had forgotten it, forgotten it completely, didn't think about it anymore. I was living proof of that, sitting there calmly smoking my second cigarette, enjoying it, watching the burning ember on its tip, allowing myself to be completely absorbed in watching it so as not to let my self get the best of me and drive me to my natural tendency to question and be anxious and afraid and impatient. The easiest thing for me now, while in that state, would have been to let myself be devoured by questions. Then by fear, then consternation, or maybe anger—and why not?—and after that, rebellion.

There were ample preconditions for that, for a hasty person at least. But what did I have to do with all of this? What did such matters, which didn't appeal to me in the least, have to do with me? What was I, there in that place, but a passerby whose passing would not take very long? What was my presence there but a mistake resulting from good intentions? Rather, what was it but a fateful coincidence? What was it but a short time that would be spent, after which the waters would return to their regular course, and I would leave that place, gush out into the streets, flow down them like water, in whatever direction I wanted, with total freedom, and with a clear conscience, not having hurt anyone or been hurt by anyone.

It's just wonderful! To get caught in a bad experience and then get out of it white as snow and be made to discover for yourself that freedom is splendid and innocence is an inexpressible joy. It's just wonderful to live moments of intense emotion that stay with you your whole life.

That old adage is true: every cloud has a silver lining.

Every time I noticed that I was delighting in nice thoughts to distract myself from bad thoughts I felt very happy. It was a sign I had a firm grip on the reins of my life and my self, a sign I was innocent, with an innocence untainted by anything inside me that could lead to anxiety or pessimism. It is well known that if something is bothering you, you can't possibly keep it hidden for very long, and nothing was bothering me. So what was there to stop me from enjoying myself, if only to the small degree permitted by the circumstances and within the limits of social etiquette, of course, by which I mean the proper behavior required when finding oneself accidentally and wrongly (I mean by coincidence) in a place other than one's own home. So let me smoke in peace then, for no one would blame me for it, and no one would consider it against the rules. I continued smoking with more and more clearness of conscience, then, and consequently more and more enjoyment, insomuch as I had begun, out of the intensity with which I succumbed to total bliss, to consider my closed eyes a blessing and a grace, until I suddenly noticed that the ash of this cigarette had now gotten very long, and of course it must have. This startled me a little, because the ashtray problem had come back and presented itself again with authority. (Strange how I kept switching from state to state and from mood to mood, in a flash!) Then I noticed a much more serious matter, which was that when I smoked for the second time, I had done it without making the decision to do so. It had been a completely spontaneous, unconscious undertaking—and this was exactly its danger. Why, after all, had I started smoking before coming up with a solution to the ashtray problem— even a theoretical solution—like saying, for example, I'll let it go out on its own like the first cigarette, on the glass desktop. Man's baser self no doubt incites evil. And now, and once again, my self had gotten me into another predicament. I had to take action immediately. I had to find a quick solution. And that's what stole me away from savoring my cigarette, which I was thoroughly enjoying to the point of total bliss. (Too bad, because it was really a beautiful moment.) Then I figured why not put it on the desk and let it go out on its own once I'm finished smoking it? But that would only solve the immediate problem, whereas the first problem, the primary problem, would remain, in all it weightiness, unsolved: how could I have acted without first deciding to!

"Oh vile self!" ← "Oh vile tongue"

I know people make mistakes. Indeed, I know that making

mistakes is a human characteristic. But don't you dare make one when the interrogators, or the questioners, or the examiners, or the inquisitors come (after all, what good-hearted name should I call them after having spent so much time there), because a mistake then would be fatal. Or, in other even franker terms, it would be deadly. (I apologize for being so frank.)

"Yes."

Just because a mistake is permissible in one situation or another, it doesn't mean it is permissible always—meaning any time and anywhere—so how could it be permissible now, in such a delicate situation where truth was as easy as water, could be colored easily and by showing good intentions could please the interrogator, could be formed accordingly, especially if it was something deep inside, especially if it was something that had happened in the past—an event of some sort. And there I was in that place because of something serious that had happened, if seen from the point of view of those hurt by it, or rather, if seen from a neutral position. I saw that picture with my own eyes when I was coming out of the shop, and it was torn, whereas when I had seen it only moments earlier when I was entering the shop, there was nothing wrong with it. The way it was torn suggested the worst intentions; it suggested there were strong, repressed feelings of hatred for it and whatever or whomever it represented. The picture had been glued securely to the wall and wouldn't rip the way the perpetrator wanted, at the eyes for example, so he scraped it with a knife or some sharp object, making the eyes look gouged-out and scary, and over the upper lip he etched a contemptuous line. The strange thing about the incident was that the whole thing happened in just a few, quick seconds.

I myself even wondered if the perpetrator had had some prior training. Otherwise, how could he have done it with such skill and efficiency? When I entered the shop, there had been no other customers inside. I didn't have to wait in line or anything. I got a pack of Marlboro's from the shop owner, paid, and left. Such an operation doesn't take more than a few seconds, or let's say a minute or two at the most. That means the act had been intentional and planned out in detail. The work of professionals with a foolproof plan. Otherwise, how could such a serious act take place amid such dangers, in broad daylight, and during the busiest hours of the day no less, just before noon, and not a cloud in the sky to cast even a shadow over anything. How could it happen without anyone noticing anything!

At the very least, such an act meant defiance.

Therefore, the situation would not tolerate any give and take, and this is only natural. When someone wants to push you out of the way, for example, in order to take your place, and does it in such a manner, it's only logical for you not to be forgiving and kind to him and willingly give up your place. Or, when someone wants to insult you in such a manner, you're not expected to treat him nicely, because the insult is unfounded no matter what the point of contention might have been or how important, because the instigator in this case would "skin you alive" if he were able, as people say.

In truth I perceived all these facets right away. I mean as soon as I left the store and saw the picture was torn. And my perception had been spontaneous, instinctive. I mean, I didn't think of the matter consciously and clearly. Rather, it had been a kind of animal intuition, which might never have surfaced into consciousness had I not been dragged to this place where

I now was. And that was exactly what scared me. I mean, that unconscious animal feeling, which was now turning into pure consciousness, taking over my whole psyche, and making me appear before my very own eyes as though I had something to do with it all, being so knowledgeable about it as I was, and so knowledgeable about the parts of it that were concealed and the parts that weren't and what its consequences would be. What was scary, really scary, was that this "knowledge" (necessarily?) might show in my actions and I might surprise myself in front of the investigators and leak it out. Then I would be caught in a predicament that would consume my entire lifetime, even if I still had a few years left when it was over. That was why from the moment I had gotten into that mess, I watched myself carefully, trying always not to allow any movement without prior consideration, down to the minutest detail, to avoid making a fatal mistake. For sure, I knew that the task I had placed before myself was extremely difficult, more like impossible, but there in that room I understood for the first time in my life that if you don't realize the impossible, nothing is possible. Only by realizing the impossible could everything go on as it had before, in other words, could I be saved. For this reason, and in simplest terms, I had to find an ashtray, or find a solution to the problem of the ashes and the cigarette butt, one way or another. This was the immediate problem being presented to me at that moment, because the cigarette ash had gotten very long and I couldn't wait for the light to come back on; that might be too late. While waiting to come up with an adequate solution to that problem I flicked the ash of the cigarette I was smoking onto the carpet and rubbed it in with my foot like the first time, so any evidence of it would disappear into the fibers. As for the cigarette butt,

I placed it as before on the desk and let it breathe and dim down until it went out. When it went out I shut my eyes and said to myself: <u>I will not allow my self to surprise me again. I will not be driven again unexpectedly to do anything, no matter how insignificant it might be or seem to be.</u>

(Maybe the lights came back on.)

When I opened my eyes after having shut them nothing had changed except that the dark, when you open your eyes to it, is upsetting. It is like a blockade and you feel afraid your eyes might bump into something, so you shut them again and finally adjust to it little by little.

Light had truly been a blessing, and it always is, of course, no matter what kind of light it is, electric or sunlight. Really, a person doesn't know the value of something until it's gone. Anyway, I didn't care what kind of light it was except to the extent that it had some connection to the nature of the place I had suddenly found myself in. I mean that from the kind of light it was I thought I could infer the nature of the room I was in, and consequently the mistake, or the misunderstanding, or the "accusation" that made them take me there; for, if it was sunlight, then my situation was less "serious," since a person under arrest, or a dangerous criminal, is not put into a room that receives sunlight from a window unprotected by metal bars. As for someone put in a closed-up place where no sunlight can enter, the charge against him calls for it. Unless... unless they had a shortage of places, or there was some other reason to put him there, and that was my case for sure. I was convinced of that.

In simplest terms I was convinced I had been put there in that place by chance. Chance forced them to put me there, not the nature of the accusation, and therefore I was relaxed and at ease and my nerves were calm. Otherwise, how could you explain my strong desire for the moment to finally arrive when someone would come to me so I could declare the truth to him, without an inkling of a shadow of a doubt around it, with sparkling clarity, eliciting from him an embarrassed smile that expressed a feeling of "guilt" he would like to forget. This, now, was precisely the issue: for someone to come and check on me. My biggest and greatest fear was that the person who had led me to the room didn't inform anyone about me, or his superior was absent, or I was just one of those insignificant matters that hamper the regular flow of life and which, because of their insignificance, don't deserve a moment's attention. I hated to think he might be on vacation—on some trip somewhere, to give an example. No! I didn't want to consider that possibility. It would destroy me totally no matter how firm my confidence in my own innocence was. Then it wouldn't be them I was afraid of, since they wanted to know the truth, and the truth would mean my freedom. Rather, I would be afraid of my own self, of the possibility of losing control of my self, thus being led to ruin by a mistake I would make in spite of myself. And if that were to happen, it wouldn't be the first time. Indeed, I had gotten hurt so many times I was used to it. The hours in which God forsakes us, which the faithful call "the hours of abandonment," and during which we unwillingly make mistakes, come to me repeatedly, so often that they don't even surprise me anymore, no matter how bad the outcome is for me. In fact, with time I've developed an ability to alleviate some of the harm. I have gotten very good at apologizing, for example. I'm the master of apology, and I've gotten so skillful at being peaceable that I've become famous for it. That's because a hurt person always greets the gentle person's apology with an open heart, and because any harm that comes at the hand of a meek person is never intentional. Such harm might even lead to a deepening of the friendship between the harmed and the offender, turning dissension into an opportunity for greater understanding.

I've become addicted to revealing the truth in order to show my innocence and beg off misunderstandings.

Yes, I call it an addiction because it is that and nothing else.

In turn, this addiction to revealing the truth has become part of me and without it I can't maintain my sense of balance, so I end up seeking out the kinds of problems that call for it.

But what was happening now was totally, totally different. Who was going to accept my apology with affection and love? Who was going to speak heart to heart with me so we could remedy the misunderstanding between us? Here life wasn't the same as life among friends, or among people of the same community. Here a mistake meant something, and harm meant something, and everything was taken into account. "*C'est normal.*"

But while on that subject, I was not saying all this about my usual difficulties with my self in order to blame it for my being there, because my self was not responsible. And if it was absolutely necessary to determine who was responsible, I could only say it was chance. Chance was what had gotten me there. If, on the other hand, I insisted on blaming myself, then there must be something wrong with me. I must have some kind of flaw, no doubt about it. But fortunately I did not insist—in fact, quite the contrary. I insisted upon my innocence.

But just because I didn't blame my self for my being there, that didn't mean at all that I didn't blame my self for all the mistakes I had made, one after the other, starting the moment the door to that room was locked shut on me, because it had become clear that these mistakes, which seemed small, were going to cost me a lot. And even if I had managed to reduce their effects, I wasn't one hundred percent sure what would happen next. What kind of assurance was there in assuming that I wouldn't surprise myself in the event that their boss was off on vacation somewhere (out of the country?) or on some urgent mission, and break down the door, for example, or pound it with my fists loud enough to bother everyone in the building. And this, all this when the very thing I needed to do, the very thing, was to leave my mind in charge of matters and behave according to what it thought and according to its logic. And reason was saying that staying there, waiting politely and respectfully, and with complete comprehension of the circumstances that had led them to "detain" me, was the only way I would get out quickly (as quickly as possible) and with my dignity intact. Otherwise I would be forced to face a situation there was no guarantee I could get out of. Reason was saying: I might have to wait hours, maybe the whole day (and it would be more correct to say the rest of the day, because nearly half of it was already gone.) I might have to stay there all night. So what? That wasn't a disaster. A disaster would be to lose my patience. That would be a disaster. What, after all, were a few hours spent outside a person's regular routine? Who doesn't run into such situations some time in his life? Who, for example, doesn't get into some accident? Who doesn't run his car into something and then have to waste long hours getting it fixed? Who doesn't wind up spending a few days in the hospital, if not more, for some accidental, silly reason? Getting the water back on because you left the faucet open and the water running while you were out—would force you to spend hours fixing it.

trying so hard to normalize detainment

If you forget your house key, you end up spending the whole night out on the street like a bum until the next morning.

And who's never had their washing machine quit working, or the refrigerator, or something much sillier than that, like the water faucet. How much time and effort does that take up? A headache can cause a person to waste an entire day. The common cold paralyzes a person—no exaggeration—several weeks out of the year.

The point of all this is that what I was in was not a disaster or anything out of the ordinary, but merely a common situation, even if it didn't happen every day. So I should see things reasonably—the word is clear: reasonably—and I should stop blowing things out of proportion. Patience, patience, nothing but patience. Patience is a virtue no matter what negative things might be said about it. No one has ever regretted being patient the way he or she might regret having been hasty, and I am patient by nature. I like that about myself, and I like it when friends and acquaintances describe me that way. So what on earth came over me and changed me now? Why? Right when what I needed was the exact opposite. That is, to just be myself. Just be myself! That first decision I made—to be natural and not just seem natural—was a smart and correct decision. The situation still demanded that I hold it to the letter, in form and in meaning. That side of my nature was exactly what must control my actions, now while they were away as well as later when they came back, in case their attention was drawn to something I was ready to clear up, like the smell of smoke in the room. I would go ahead and clarify it without hesitation and completely naturally. Smoking was one of my bad habits that I could not, unfortunately, stop. My hope in this was that my conversant not be the wrong type and say something like,

"And what other bad habits do you have?"—meaning by that the torn picture and implying I was the one who did it.

"Please, tell us all about these habits."

I should prepare some other answer, then. One that would not lead me into such a trap. Something shorter, less vulnerable, like, "I'm a smoker."

But then again, he could still answer with something like, "God forgive you! Smoking is bad for you. Why do you squander away your health when you need it with your whole future ahead of you?"—meaning by that that he assumes I was the one who tore the picture out of a desire I had to push them aside so I could take their place.

The answers would have to be studied carefully. Answering off the cuff would be very costly. Moreover, studying the answers would not be contrary to the naturalness I had to maintain at all costs, even if it—studying that is—might take away some of the randomness of my answers, or better, the spontaneity. But that was not totally correct. Quick thinking and smarts were not at all opposed to being natural. Therefore, my well-studied answers would just have to appear spur of the moment, and completely natural. To appear...

To *appear*...!

But I could make them *be* natural, by repeating them over and over... dozens of times per answer. But the problem was that even if I could guess many of the questions in advance, it would be impossible to guess all of them. And let's suppose I could guess them all, it would require a lot of time—maybe days, or weeks—before I could naturalize them. (I mean make them natural.)

The solution?

The solution had to be based on the premise that the

questions must be studied. That was obvious, because a mistake was impermissible.

Then the simplest solution was to start at the beginning. In other words, with the simple, tangible, and visible matters. I should begin by listing all the movements I made since entering that place and then prepare answers to every possible related question. Why did I sit down, stand up, proceed to the window, bump into the table, smoke, and so on. Let's start with the ashtray, since it now was the most pressing matter, and since the cigarette between my fingers was now down to the end.

The cigarette was down to the end, so what should I do with it? I didn't hesitate very long before putting it on the desk. Then, while watching the ember as it panted humbly, I tried to figure out a substitute for the absent ashtray, and it occurred to me to put the cigarette butts in the cuff of my pant leg. Why not? There was enough room in it to hold an entire pack of cigarette butts. So be it. I groped around in that all-encompassing darkness for the cigarette butts I had put on the desk. I picked up the first one, and with firm determination—so it wouldn't fall and get away from me—I tucked it into the cuff of my left pant leg. And then, just as I was reaching for the second cigarette butt, the phone rang!

The phone rang and ruined everything.

I had been sitting down, but when the phone rang I nearly flew up off of the couch, and it seemed like a few seconds passed before I realized I landed; though I didn't know where.

The worst part of it all was the stress the noise caused to my brain.

And then it rang again!

The darkness, as I have already described it, was entirely and completely unyielding.

Then the phone rang a third time. I remained where I was, right where I had landed after the first ring, not moving a muscle, waiting with full-blown anticipation and readiness for the next ring—the next ring whose time had come. But it didn't ring. And it still didn't ring. There was that pressure on my brain like before and more, and then finally it was too late: the phone had stopped ringing. It only rang three times.

After I made sure the phone stopped ringing, I noticed my heart was beating horribly fast. And it hurt, as if a hundred needles were poking it. I was breathing hard, too, and couldn't catch my breath. I was dripping with sweat and the various spots on my body that hurt were too many to count. It felt like someone was attacking me with the kinds of instruments a surgeon or a dentist uses.

It seems that when the phone rang the first time, when I was groping for the cigarette butts and then suffered that sudden shock and got so shaken up, I must have lost all control of myself and spontaneously backed away from the source of the sound next to me on the desk just to my left. I must have backed away with unusual speed, and no doubt in some undetermined direction.

I say all this must have happened to me, because I didn't know exactly where I had landed, or in what position. I wasn't sitting exactly, nor was I standing. For sure I was lying on my back, and my legs were up on something or other, raised up. My head began to hurt, my whole head, especially my forehead, on the right side, possibly just over my eye, or possibly the eye itself, as if someone had punched it with his fist. I felt a lukewarm liquid flowing over it, so I shut my eye, but it didn't respond to me the way it usually does. I wasn't sure if it was shut or not. I felt the liquid flow down to my ear and start to pool up inside it. The liquid was blood, no doubt about it. Figuring that out didn't require a whole lot of intelligence. I was wounded, therefore, but I didn't know how serious the injury was. I was alive, though, that much I could tell. And I had full control of my mental faculties. I could move, but willfully refrained from it in order to ascertain what little I could of the severity of the injury. (Really, the first aid skills we learn in school or pick up here and there show how crucial they are in situations like the one I was now in, and the indispensable benefits of learning them become very clear.)

It felt like someone was twisting one of my legs really hard! Like my leg was wrapped around itself—my leg, which certainly is no rope or any other pliable thing. I couldn't even tell anymore if it was my right leg or my left or both, because pain dulls the senses. I seemed to be lying on broken glass, because every time I moved, thousands of little slivers poked into me. My hands went completely dead, as if they were tied securely to the wall or something like a wall. So I waited like that, involuntarily, patiently bearing out the pain and waiting for my head to clear so I could figure out how I had gotten into that condition. After a while I was able to recall what must have happened. When I reacted suddenly in my attempt to "get away" from the phone after it rang all of a sudden, I bumped into the table in the middle of the room, that table that was basically a metal bench with a pane of glass on top. The glass, therefore, shattered and pieces of it scattered all over the place, some of them landing where I fell. As for the paralysis I felt in my hands, well maybe it resulted from serious lacerations, but I didn't know why it felt like my legs were raised above the rest of my body, and at the same time as if they were twisted up like pliant tree branches.

Then, in a moment of clarity, as if I'd forgotten all my pain, it suddenly occurred to me that the phone call might have been for me. Yes, it had been for me! They wanted to tell me something.

Maybe they wanted to let me know I could leave. Most likely. Indeed, that was the purely logical thing. Or maybe, in the worst case scenario, they wanted to tell me they were coming, or they wanted to summon me. Logic insisted to me that they certainly did not want me to rot there forever. I couldn't see how that could possibly benefit them.

Oh, if only I had remained ignorant of that!

If only it hadn't occurred to me that the call was for me, and that the chance I had waited so long for had slipped away.

Oh, God!

Start all over again?

Again I would have to wait. I was right back where I started, or maybe further back. What was worse, now the caller surely thought I wasn't there anymore and he was consequently rid of me. As far as he was concerned the case was closed. Now who was going to remember I was still there? Indeed, who was going to remember I even existed at all, especially since the room I was in was completely forgotten, so it seemed, the way no one ever came into it. And what was that damned room, anyway? What was its nature, its purpose? Where was it with respect to the light, with respect to the sunlight? I had to know about the place in order to understand how they viewed me. I know I was not in some covered hole, but rather a very nice place in which I could stretch out and sleep if I wanted. So what kind of place was it? This was a fundamental question, in fact the basis for everything else. The answer to it would clarify the nature of my being there. I had to move in that direction, but how?

v could I move in that direction when I was in that strange and unexpected position? My first concern had to be to stop the bleeding right away. I **was** bleeding from all directions—my forehead, my back, possibly my hands, and possibly my legs. Then it all seemed like a dream, as if I were seeing a lit cigarette moving about in the darkness, the way it might move if held by an invisible hand. It was as though I was dreaming, and it wouldn't be unusual for a person to dream in such a stressful situation, which creates an urgent need to dream as a means of escape from bitter reality, as a way of symbolically conquering it. And the cigarette burned me when it touched against me from time to time, as if the hand holding it was completely unaware of my presence in that place, or unaware of my exact location in that place, and just moved about anywhere it wanted without caring one bit who might be watching, landing most unfortunately on the places on my body that were already hurting, especially my eye, where it struck repeatedly, as if my eye was the thing it wanted to hit most, leaving it only to return moments later. Each time it would come back from a different direction, once from the right, next from the left, then from above, but always, always, to my eye.

And why always the eye and not the fingers, for example, like the index finger and thumb of my right hand, where it would also land from time to time as it roamed?

It was as if I were dreaming.

It was as if I were dreaming of a lit cigarette that approached my upper lip just where my moustache would be, and tiptoed across it, or of something sharp slashing at that spot. That reminded me of the picture and how the perpetrator slashed it when he was unable to tear it off the wall, and the similarities made me smile.

It was as if, while lying there on the broken glass, bleeding from all directions…

It was as if I were dreaming someone was there beside me, consoling me with his presence, no matter how much he was hurting me, for I had an undeniable need for company in that melancholy darkness, and in that strange position I didn't know how to get out of.

I should have answered the phone!

I should have answered the phone instead of allowing myself to get into that position—somewhere in that room, covered with blood, unable to do anything.

These were the fruits of random action.

These were the fruits of spontaneous, unplanned action.

Now everything had changed because of this reckless act. Nothing was the same anymore, and thus it was necessary for me to get things back under control, and quickly. I had to take small, specific steps, steps planned with infinite precision, but within a finite period of time that must not be too quick. (I must not forget that speed and hastiness are not the same thing.)

But, was this possible now, after what had happened?

I said before that the impossible was the only possibility now. I had no other choice. The impossible was the only way left. I had to study every step I planned to take with infinite precision, and then each step had to be taken precisely too, without hesitation. Quickly, but with speed, not haste. Okay, then, but where should I begin? The situation was fundamentally different now, so I should proceed with this simple and basic concept in mind. But that dream, which had started to transform into a nightmare, still had a hold on me. That cigarette was still moving about on its own, as if by invisible fingers, and still touched me from time to time as it moved, on sensitive parts of my body, especially my eye, poking me harder and harder, and I was still lying on the broken glass, bleeding, my leg raised up, and my hands still in their sorry state, as if I had yielded myself to some primitive torture. But the pain I was experiencing must call me to take action rather than surrender. I must begin immediately, quickly. (I repeat: speed is not haste.) But how?

How should I start?

I was thirsty!

And I think I became thirsty for one of two reasons: either from loss of blood, or because I had dreamed of drinking, or maybe for both reasons. And why not?

The water I drank in my dream didn't taste like any water I had ever drunk before. Maybe that's why I got thirsty for cold, fresh water.

It was as though the water I drank was mixed with different kinds of strange-tasting medicines, like in the hospital.

The strange-tasting water seemed to smell familiar, and feel familiar, more salty than not, tending toward room temperature. How strange dreams are!

It gushed into my mouth from somewhere in the middle. At times I felt it go into my nostrils and reach my eyes and flow over my face in all directions. So maybe it was the perfect cure for my wounds, sprinkled upon me by some unseen divine providence. (Urine is an old folk remedy for cuts and insect bites.)

Really, I had to get out of that unbecoming position right away. I had to begin with something other than wasting time trying to figure out what to start with. So let me just start with the first thing that came to mind. I was such a fool! What a dimwit I was! All that time I had been wondering and wondering what to start with, when all along it had been as

[margin note: did he pee or did a Soldier?]

54

obvious as the sweeping anger I felt at not being able to see. First I had to get up, before anything else! Did it make any sense to try and do anything while lying there like a mule that wouldn't budge?

If only the earth would swallow me up!

rep If only the earth would crack open, swallow me into its belly, and make me disappear forever! And so, I sat up.

As simple as that, I sat up, and with a piece of cloth that somehow found its way to my hand (or my hand somehow found it) I wiped my eyes first, or at least I tried to, because they hurt so much I couldn't really wipe them. Then I wiped... I wiped what I could, and what could I do, really, with blood all over me everywhere, and using only one hand because the other one was still being held by some unknown, unshakable, and unyielding thing. My foot was still raised up. Strange! How could my leg be raised up if I was sitting! I attempted to get up but couldn't. I tried again unsuccessfully, and realizing that I had to do something about my leg or I would never be able to get up, I came up with a strategy. I reached with my free hand to my leg and felt it carefully down to my foot, which was without a shoe. My shoe had fallen off in the commotion. How was I going to stand up and walk on the floor when there was broken glass all over it? This was a new problem, and I didn't blame myself for not foreseeing it. The bigger surprise, though, was that my other foot was also shoeless. It had all happened in that cursed moment of chaos, which could instead have been my moment of salvation. What a paradox. The very same thing could be either this or that! Why didn't I answer the phone? What is it that makes us commit such deadly mistakes? What is that region of the soul that decides our actions? And how? And why this action and not that? I know we shouldn't try to understand the hidden and the obscure, but what was it exactly in that region of my soul that determined that particular decision?

Hey man, forget philosophy now. This is not the time. Now is the time for serious thinking and action, so make the right decision for this moment and carry it out with precision.

The next thing I realized was that I was actually wearing my shoes. I was not shoeless as I had imagined, but I felt I had no socks on, or seemed to have no socks on, but that was merely an insignificant detail. I headed in that stubborn darkness toward the couch and sat down. Ah!

I sighed to myself: ah! But not out of relief; I was still in a lot of pain. I sighed only because I had sat down, nothing more. At least this was a presentable position, and one from which I could face things differently, with much more ease and balance. In this position it also forced others, even if subconsciously, to treat you like a human being, like a person. As for the pain, it was getting worse. I had been expecting it to subside some when I sat on the couch, but I was wrong. The pain was still live, and growing stronger. When I say "live" pain, I mean the kind that attacks you right at the core, right in the very nerves of your heart, or the very heart of your nerves; the thing on which your very existence rests. Live pain flashes before your eyes as if somehow separate from you completely, like a spear or a bolt of lightning, clear and unequivocal, now a sudden pang, now a constant ache, and you all the while in total darkness. Despite all this, however, I had to forget the pain. I had to overcome it in order to be saved. I had to overcome my pain. It was the only possible way. Do the impossible! That was exactly what had to be done, exactly what I had to do. Anything short of that would be empty words, a waste of time. I had to act now, immediately, without delay. God knows I had wasted enough time already. "Enough!" I don't know why this English word suddenly came to mind, especially since I don't know much English at all, and what little I do know I don't know how to use properly.

"Act! Don't waste more time on nonsense! What you must do now is obvious, and it's a lot to do: clean up the bits of glass from all over the floor; pick up all the cigarette butts from the desk; straighten up all the chaos that was stirred up and left behind by the "storm." Okay, I would start with the easy job—picking up the cigarette butts.

So I began. I felt around with my hand until it fell upon the butt from my second cigarette, which I had been groping for earlier when the phone rang and startled me and caused the subsequent immense damages. I grabbed it and put it in my pant cuff as I had done earlier with the first cigarette butt, which unfortunately was no longer there. No doubt it had fallen out during the "storm," and now in that darkness there was no way of uncovering its whereabouts; most likely it was somewhere among the broken glass and therefore finding it would have to be postponed and taken up later along with the issue of the broken glass itself.

Then I found the third cigarette butt, as quickly and easily as I had found the second, and placed it in the cuff of my pant leg. Afterwards I felt a certain satisfaction; it is so nice to work at something and reap the fruits of your labor. I wanted to do as the ad says and "crown my pleasure with a Marlboro," but when I searched my jacket pockets for the pack of cigarettes.... It seemed that the shock over the phone ringing not only caused heavy damages, it had been a veritable disaster. This is what I discerned with the passing of time.

Where had the pack of cigarettes fallen to? And a pack of cigarettes calls for a lighter, so where was the lighter?

It appeared that matters were moving decidedly away from my will, from my ability to control them. Should I surrender?

Should I continue sitting there on that couch, waiting, one leg crossed over the other, just letting things happen as they would, like someone in absolute despair, or someone who couldn't possibly care any less? The electricity was back on.

The electricity was back on!

Yes! It was the electricity without a doubt. That was clear, because the sun does not appear and disappear; it just stays on the course that was set for it at the beginning of time. Electricity on the other hand comes and goes. But the difference between light from this thing called electricity and light from the sun is ever so slight, to the point that it's impossible to tell the two apart. Strange! Never in my whole life had any light caused me so much confusion as that light that day. But how? Was it possible for someone living in an area of the world like ours—where the sun is a treasure and symbolizes pride, clarity, and where every citizen knows it to be a gift bestowed upon us by the heavens above—to confuse sunlight with electric light?

At any rate, after I got over the shock of the electricity coming back on, I noticed that my vision was not quite right. Blurred a little maybe. No, definitely. I could not see clearly in fact, not even with both my eyes, nor could I open them all the way; there was something pressing down on my eyelids from above, preventing them from opening. But I knew it was electric light, even if I wasn't seeing clearly, and even if the atmosphere was clouded with smoke from the cigarettes I had smoked earlier. Yes, the trickle of light I was able to make out

58

was draped in a thick, black cloud of white, but the intriguing thing was that this cloud of smoke could not possibly have been produced by the few cigarettes I had smoked. Such a cloud would require several smokers to produce it—three or four at least. So who had been smoking with me! Or had the room been full of smoke before I even arrived, but I hadn't noticed because of the hasty way everything happened? Whatever the case, I had to open something, a door, or a window, or a hole of some sort, or else I would suffocate. I had nearly suffocated already. I made a decision to get up, go to the door, and open it, knowing the door would be the one sure thing I would be able to open. I say sure thing because I had seen it opened, and had seen it closed behind me. Indeed I had entered through it when I came in. I stood up now with this resolve and headed toward the door confidently and naturally. I reached for the doorknob with my hand, took hold of it in order to open...

"The mind is a treasure!"

"The mind is a treasure!" This is what older folks say when someone does something heedless, or hasty, or childish.

I grabbed hold of the doorknob in order to open the door...

"Come on! From the beginning! Don't get yourself into another mess you could do without. Recall again your whole day, starting with the moment you woke up. What did you do? Where did you go? Who did you call? Who did you meet? What did you hear? What did you see? And odors, too, might be of significance. Who knows? Come on!"

Okay, yes, so how did my day begin?

My day began as usual, like every morning.

How exactly does a day begin as usual, like every morning? What does that mean exactly, and of what use is it to someone asking who is completely empty-headed? What use is it to someone asking about who I am, the way I live, the nature of the things that occupy me day and night?

But if I really wanted to recall my entire day, it would take me an eon. The best thing would be to start with the most important things, then move on to the important things if there was time, and then touch on the least important. How to measure importance was clear: what mattered was what mattered to them, and what mattered to them was just as clear: anything and everything that aroused their suspicions toward me.

So what went on during this day of mine, starting first thing in the morning, that would give them reason to question?

Nothing.

"Come on, wise ass. You've babied your memory enough, now put it to work. Don't worry, hard work won't ruin it! So now, who did you run into? Who did you call? Who did you meet with? Which of them is suspicious, or might be considered suspicious?"

Oh, that name that I forgot!

The name of the man I ran into before entering the store, the one I tried to address by name but couldn't because his name had simply slipped my mind.

Yes, I forgot his name.

I had tried in vain at the time to remember, which really upset me (it always upsets me, because I always attribute that to aging) and this was very obvious, because he asked me what was the matter, was I worried about something? "No, no," I said. "Everything is fine."

But now it was very serious. I had to remember. Had to. It was a question of life or death. I closed my eyes nearly all the way and tried to remember. I could remember his face perfectly, with total clarity; I remembered his walk, his clothes, but not his name. His name escaped me, that was all there was to it. I remembered the hair on his hands, the smile on his face, his stretched lips. How could I explain that to them? (And at the same time, how could I blame them?)

But I forgot his name.

It's the law of nature; as you get older, you start to forget things. And on top of that, I am forgetful. I've been described that way for a long time. Forgetful. And I don't know. I could be to blame for that. I never exercised my memory much, and so often I've heard that if you work your memory, it will stay active a long time, and be stronger.

But now it was imperative that I remember. There had been times before when I actually did succeed in remembering, which means such a thing wasn't impossible. Rather, it was quite possible, and since realizing the impossible had become my current goal, certainly the possible in comparison would be easy as drinking a glass of water.

I always used to bump into him from time to time, and greet him excitedly. He in turn harbored feelings of affection and friendship for me. I've known him for a long time and there's never been an occasion in which his name was mentioned that I didn't immediately remember who he was. In the same vein, I never thought for a moment that I would ever forget his name; yes, it had been a long time since I had used it. I didn't even remember the last time I said it, or who I was with. It's strange, the kinds of friendships that get woven together between you and people you know nothing about, except that when you see them, you're happy, you smile spontaneously, and greet them with the traditional, mechanical, nice expressions exclusive to such occasions, then you leave them and they you, only to run into them again somewhere after a time—could be long, could be short—and greet them once again the same way.

I tried and tried stubbornly to remember his name, to avoid being embarrassed by having forgotten. (Oh, if only the matter could be reduced to mere embarrassment.) Many names came to mind that I thought were his but weren't. Many names came to mind that seemed to me to suit him and therefore might actually be his name; some suited his smile, or his bashfulness, or the way he talked, or his gentle nature.

His gentle nature. How was it possible that he, the gentle one, was the very thing, intentionally or not, that was putting me in so much danger?

While I thought about him in this manner his face would appear to me, suggesting... could it be? Could he have had something to do with it? I had run into him just before reaching the door of the store, in front of the picture. In fact, he had turned his face toward it for just a second (as far as I remember), but what had been his role? Tearing it, or setting me up? No. No way! What right did I have to blame him for the consequences of my bad memory?

But was his name going to get me in trouble?

Maybe they had been keeping surveillance over the area when I stopped to greet him. Maybe they took pictures. Maybe what I would call saying hello, they would call passing secret information, or conspiring. That was their right, after all, to think what they wanted, suppose whatever they wanted; it was their job. No one could blame them for that. The solution to this particular problem from its very basis lay with me and me alone. They had a right to know. I owed it to them. So what was his name? As soon as they knew that, they could conduct a thorough investigation on him, if they wanted, and find out if the information I had given them was correct. And, really, who would believe anyone could greet someone with such enthusiasm and yet not know his name?

Oh, what's his name what's his name what's his name. Oh God! Oh god of memory! Wasn't there a god of memory I could appeal to for help? All I could remember was his smile, his smiling face. But then even that disappeared or got erased and turned into other faces, while I went on concentrating on it so hard I felt something swell up and get ready to explode inside my head. I tried to put it all out of my mind for a little while to give myself a break. Then I started all over again with renewed enthusiasm and motivation, but all in vain. I tried to sleep a little, in order to wake up afterwards fresh and bright— nature goes about its tasks calmly and efficiently during sleep—but I was still in a lot of pain from all the nearly life-threatening damage the storm had caused me. I would resume concentrating on his name, then, trying to coax it to me from another angle. I would use another approach, such as starting with the bit of it I did remember and trying to leap from there onto the rest of the name. Or, I would start with the shape of his face, his smile, the way his lips were stretched widely into a smile, his sunken eyes upon his smiling face smiling face smiling face... I had it... I had it... Yes, God... No! I didn't have it. The name didn't come, or else the name that did come wasn't the right one. I kept trying until finally my heart sank and stopped beating and those hard, pointy things pierced it and stuck there and multiplied.

At times I would forget what I had remembered, so I would try to remember what it was I forgot, especially if I felt that what I forgot was close to the goal—close to the name.

can't remember
due to panic of
torture?

Remembering the remembered—that was an exhausting, stifling, unending procedure.

That was it. It was over. I couldn't do it. There was no way. Couldn't be done. Finished. I would be better off saving the strength I was wasting on trying to remember, for handling what was to come, though exactly what that was no one knew—how severe, of what nature, how effective would it be, how long would it last, what would be its outcome.

I would get back to it later.

Or maybe it would come by itself, by chance, the way such things often do. That was why I should switch to doing something else now.

Yes, indeed, that something else!

That something you simply can't avoid, and which no use of trickery can succeed in putting off. In vain did I try to keep lying to myself. It was useless; lying to yourself does not convince others.

Now I believe that the real reason I concentrated on trying to remember his name might have been to avoid switching to doing that other thing. My address book. Oh, if only I could swallow it up.

Is there anyone in this world who possesses an address book who hasn't been shocked at one time or another to open his own address book and find lots of names, clearly written in his own handwriting, belonging to people he couldn't remember at all? For a long time now I had known that my address book contained names of people I couldn't remember the slightest thing about, nor did I remember when I wrote the names or on what occasion. There were even names I couldn't read! Maybe I had written them in a hurry, or in a car, or standing up. Some names weren't clear—they had been erased, or written in pencil or with a pen that had run out of ink. But the real catastrophe was going to be when I was questioned about one full name that was written clearly and legibly. Would anyone believe me if I answered "I don't know?" And this when the interrogator in such situations is persistent, stubborn, and not daunted from performing his duty by anything, any trick, or anyone. In fact, he would have been hired specifically for having such characteristics, which he in turn would have improved and developed in order to gain the attention and approval of his superiors, thereby making it possible for himself to advance up the ranks.

I was always telling myself I should buy a new address book and copy into it only the numbers I always used. But now, *il est trop tard.* So, why not eat it? It was small enough, and lightweight; the only difficult part would be the cover, but in principle I could do it, with enough water!

Water? Where was I supposed to get water from?

If I could just chew it up and swallow it, everything would be all right. I would save myself from a big, big problem that might lead me into a predicament I couldn't handle. Okay. Let me do it. Oh God. But if I started, I would have to finish, or else I would be merely be moving out from under a drip only to stand beneath the eaves as they say. I had to eat it down to the last scrap. Not leave a trace, or else I would be giving them clear proof of my guilt. And so I began with the first page; I chewed it slowly and swallowed it. (Actually, I mean I shoved it down my throat.) It was no easy matter, but as I've said over and over, under the circumstances I had to achieve the impossible, so what choice did I have concerning lesser deeds?

The second page was extremely difficult. I couldn't swallow it. I should have given it more time, and I needed water, lots of water, and more water still. It was impossible otherwise. (I mean beyond my means.)

Impossible! (I mean beyond my means.)

After a while I realized that the entire address book was in my mouth. It was a moment of sheer exasperation. I had to chew and chew and chew, willingly, so as to avoid being forced. There was not a drop of saliva left in my mouth, not a trace. My mouth was totally dry, a block of wood. How was I supposed to swallow under such conditions? Especially with the first page still stuck in my throat, and the second on top of the first and everything piled up on top of it up one after the other, obstructing progress. That's life for you, one obstacle after another.

I know people, or one person at least, who would never write down names in his address book that might cause problems for him—like names of co-workers who had no connection to him other than their common desire to eke out a living on this earth. Their names were merely people's names that other people whispered back and forth. I was present once when he distorted one such name as he was writing it down, until it became some other name, so I asked him why. "Didn't you see that name?" he said. "Who would say it openly? Especially in writing! And who knows? Who knows into whose hands this piece of writing might fall, and then you'll be responsible for the consequences, because the person asking about it will want the truth, and it'll be up to you to give it to him, or up to him to get it out of you. 'The mind is a treasure.' Haven't you heard that bit of wisdom?" he asked me. "Why expose yourself to problems for no reason, *bêtement*?" After he said that he winked at me. I envy him! At least I do now. Now I envy him, though at the time I scoffed at him under my breath. In fact, I was amazed such people existed. Preposterous! I thought to myself. The man was abnormal. I envy him.

Now I envy him.

I thought about him a good long time as I strained to swallow the pages of my address book and the front and back covers. Oh, how I envied him, and imagined him coming home from work right about now—this was just the time he would be getting home. He opens the door to where his three children scramble to greet him. (He got married before me.) They surround him from all sides, making it difficult for him to decide how to greet them all, whom to pick up first. He worries his little girl will be lost in the confusion, so he picks her up first, then squats down to reach his two sons who are pulling at the legs of his pants. "Baba! Baba!" An orchestra of little voices calling "Baba! Baba!" Then he takes them all inside to where his wife, dressed comfortably, has been standing and watching them with her head bent affectionately to the side, pleasantly waiting for him to be free of the children and come to her, with a smile, or a touch, or maybe a kiss. Then he wants to make himself comfortable. First he takes off his shoes. His wife brings him his slippers unasked, then asks if he would like a drink, or doesn't ask, allowing him to take his fill of seeing the children. I am so jealous.

I am so jealous of him, the one I scoffed at under my breath. The one whose image did not leave my mind for a second as I chewed and swallowed, or tried to swallow. He was now at home with his family, and I was here.

What was I lacking that prevented me from being cautious like him? "An ounce of prevention is worth a pound of cure." That old saying is so true. Whoever made it up must have been in a situation similar to mine.

In such a situation, a person would be choking on his own saliva, so how much worse for me with what I was now trying to swallow.

Something was pulling at my throat, wrapping around it. The sides of my throat were being forced one onto the other. How difficult to have to swallow paper without water to wash it down.

The most serious thing was that there were some names in the book that truly were cause for alarm. Names belonging to people who later became involved with this person or against that person; some still were, others had changed. Some I happened to run into by coincidence somewhere, at a dinner party at a friend's house, or at some happy or sad occasion, and for some reason or another I wrote down their names and phone numbers in my address book, and there they stayed, naturally, not for any particular reason. But I never called them, or even thought about calling them. So what connection was there between them and me?

How could I explain to anyone my connection to someone I didn't remember at all, yet whose phone number I myself wrote in my personal address book; or, worse yet, how could I deny such a connection, or wash my hands of it? This really was a problem, not to mention the circumstances I was now in. If I were to put myself in the interrogator's place, how would I myself behave? Undoubtedly exactly the same way, maybe even worse. In view of what they could do and had the right to do, they were treating me humanely. Yes!

Let's be honest. Let's put personal feelings and matters aside. Can we say they were not treating me humanely? Yes, humanely!

Of course, there might be some objection to their behavior, concerning this detail or that, but such objections miss the point, no matter how relevant they might be on the personal level. The real point is, how do you justify to those bent on getting accurate information about someone, whose name they have seen with their own eyes written in your address book—how do you justify to them that you know nothing about him, or you forget who he is, or, or.... If they believed you, you yourself would be surprised.

(Isn't that right?)

For them not to believe would be logical; for them to believe would be completely illogical.

For my part, in order not to fall into this predicament, I was for swallowing the whole problem, and hiding it inside me, completely obliterating it. But I couldn't do it. It was beyond my power, and I had to bear the consequences, all of them. I accepted that without hesitation, since after all, the one thing I could be totally and absolutely sure of was that I was not going to abandon my self in those critical, oppressive moments. Impossible. Yes, it would be impossible to abandon my own self.

Those men (strange!) were extremely educated. Really, that surprised me about them. Imagine, for example, imagine that the interrogator, while you're trying to swallow the papers you chewed, says to you, "Maybe if you ruminate, you'll remember!"

That was one unusually smart thing to say.

And luck was of no help to me, either. Evil is a bottomless pit. In my address book there was one name that turned out to actually be a pseudonym. I did not know that. I swear upon everything. But what's the point of swearing. "If you're born, you're stuck." No matter how much a person tries to cleanse himself, some of the filth of this world inevitably rubs off on him. So how can a person ever be careful enough to avoid such dangerous bumps in the road? There are some lucky people, no doubt, who don't stumble into these potholes.

As for my interrogators, they had complete knowledge of everything—the actual name, the pseudonym, and why the need to create a pseudonym, too.

A person's insides are filth; his innards are filth... and when I was unable to swallow... How can I say it... How can I say it... When I was unable to swallow, which really was something beyond my capacity, I felt like something from above, from above me....

I don't exactly know why, for all intents and purposes, I was naked. I don't remember what led up to that. I don't remember at all; I totally forgot. Such forgetting is subjective, as science asserts and no one denies. It's described in medical books and everyone has heard of it and knows about it. Sometimes when a person is exposed to some kind of trauma or extremely stressful situation, he forgets completely what happened. He develops a *trou de memoire*, and is unable to remember even the tiniest detail, which might trigger memory of the event.

I know someone who was brought up by one of his relatives, and this relative liked to buy all kinds of thermometers, which he would use to take the boy's temperature several times during the day and at night, even though the boy was perfectly fine, nothing wrong with him. Nevertheless, the boy had to obey. He used to tell me how it felt. The relative used to—before I forget—make him bend over the bed, or a chair, with his feet firmly on the floor, forbidding him completely from turning back to look, and if he did, he'd slap him hard and forbid him from whimpering if it was more than he could take.

This boy (or who used to be a boy, that is) said he would get an erection, involuntarily, against his will, and against the huge

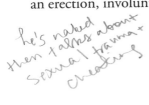
he's naked about then talks about sexual trauma + cheating

70

effort he exerted in order not to. Because he knew what consequences would ensue, in terms of encouraging and vindicating the other?

With the razor! (Me.)

In the Robert Altman film, *Short Cuts*, the doctor's wife tells her husband during a marital spat about going for a drive with another man and how they pulled over to the side of the road to have sex there inside the car. But, she assured him, he didn't come inside her. I was amazed.

I didn't actually see this movie; I read the script in French translation.

It amazed me that she would assure her husband that this other man did not come inside her. I couldn't see why it mattered if he did or didn't—the deed was done. The rest was mere details. Then I thought about it some more, trying to figure out what might be behind this assurance, especially since it had been presented with vivid details, calling things by their names, imbuing them with immediacy and fiery excitement. I reasoned that she must have told him that in order to assuage any fears he might have about AIDS, especially since the husband was a doctor, and I still believe that's why until today, or until the day what happened to me happened, I mean. And I also figured out what fundamentally motivated her: she told him in order to make an essential point, which was that their sexual intercourse had not been consummated, since he hadn't come inside her. Therefore, it could be considered, even if it were a bit of a stretch, not to have happened at all, or something along those lines, or something like that. At any rate not a firm foundation upon which to make a serious judgment. She also wanted to tell him that on the contrary, if he had come inside her, then the act would have been consummated and the situation would be completely different. It would be worth pursuing for all it was worth. In such a case, for example—had the act been consummated—he would have the right to say, "You fu—!" or, "You wh—!" or, "You cheat!" or, "You…" and behave on this basis.

It was consummated!

And right after came the razor blade, immediately after, maybe even during—that is, before it went limp.

They said I enjoyed it; you can't deny proof. (True, proof cannot be denied, but I never saw any proof, or anything else.) I had no right to protest or complain. (As for refusing, what I did was actually nothing more than complaining. I was just playing hard to get.)

"Playing hard to get, huh?"

"That was no refusal, no refusal at all; that was just complaining. Can't you see! Or is what you see here a stick? And if it is a stick, then you shouldn't feel any pain, so take this: "zap" with the razor.

"Yes. Yes. We brought you here to pleasure you."

And again and again with the razor before it went limp.

As for the pain, that would come later, when you came back to your senses. And the pain was two. Two pains.

Two places.

After that my name became "Fu—ed." Before that I didn't have any name, nor did they need for me to have a name, seeing as I was not asked about it, or about my city, or village for that matter, or my profession, or anything at all about me—about my ID card—nothing at all. This behavior, which I could not understand at all, or see the point of, completely baffled me. The name, especially in our part of the world, is half the battle, if not all of it. Without it, you have no ground to stand on. Now they had a name for me. They named me. My parents.

(I say that angrily! Honestly!)

And I say that angrily now, too. Yes, now! No one has the right to change someone else's name without his consent, or against his wishes. It was a sort of oppression I felt I was being subjected to at that moment, and I still hold the same opinion 'til today. I don't believe I'm ever going to change it.

Forgetting names is different from changing names. That's something I never get tired of saying. The two have absolutely nothing in common. Forgetting is not an insult against the person in question, as people claim. It's just forgetting and nothing more, even if often times it is embarrassing and puts the person in an undesirable position no one would envy. But my response to the notion that forgetting a person's name is equivalent to nullifying him and "X-ing" him out of existence, to annihilating him no less, my response to that is it's plain wrong. And then, why should I be blamed if it's actually—as they say—due to some subconscious desire? Judgment has never been based on intentions under any system of civil or religious law. Even religions leave the question of intentions up to God.

Really, they were educated and smart, but their education and intelligence weren't always directed toward good. In fact, their education and intelligence were exploited for other goals sometimes, due to the difficult position they were in, which would not allow for mistakes. Their primary problem was trust. Once that was solved, everything else was simple. Indeed, everything else was like nothing at all. If they had trust, then they could believe. Personally, I admit that many things about me did not inspire trust. This has to be said frankly, clearly, and unequivocally, because truthfulness is the only effective medicine in these situations, and because it is the only thing, in the end, that can rescue you from such predicaments.

I say then, truthfully and unequivocally, that I was not the model of trustworthiness in their eyes, which does not mean I was guilty, or should shoulder some responsibility, but rather it was mere chance that willed what happened. Never in my life did I think about those names written in my address book, or ask a thousand pointed questions about them—like the ones they asked me—rightfully—during my crisis. I don't blame my self for that, though, for it was chance and chance alone that willed what happened. But I learned.

Yes, I learned from this severe trial I lived through. Indeed, I learned a lot. There are things I can't possibly forget or deny, like keeping names of people I don't remember anything about written in my address book, or buying a watch like no one else's—not in terms of its quality or beauty, but its suspiciousness. Or at least in terms of eliciting all kinds of questions, sometimes sensitive questions that lead to suspicion. If even my closest friends had their doubts—yes, in a way, they had doubts, though not necessarily in the bad sense of the word, but in the innocent sense. They held suspicions, for instance, that maybe I still held my old Arab nationalist sentiments, that I hadn't yet refined these sentiments, or developed them as I should in accordance with the current international, regional, and local situation. If even my closest friends had their doubts, then how could I blame these others? These others, whose mission it was to remove all doubt and get to the truth. They were the disciples of truth, and whoever claims the contrary is either wrong or lying. They were the disciples of clarity. They were bound to face huge difficulties in

74

their efforts to get to the truth and clarify it. And so it was their right, with this as their premise—that they would always face difficulties, sometimes insurmountable difficulties that might threaten to destroy them. It was their right to stop at everything and anything that raised their doubts and strive with every means at their disposal—yes, every means—to remove that doubt and arrive at clarity. I don't deny that here lay the problem—resorting to use every means, that is, because—unfortunately—people do not answer questions with the same level of concern that controls the behavior of the interrogators. In fact, they answer with a different anxiety, which has to do with getting out of there—out of the crisis and the predicament—as soon as possible and with the least amount of damage. That's precisely the mistake, because understanding the goal of the interrogator, coupled with a little bit of cooperation, is the only and fastest road to a safe escape. That is if the people are truly innocent. As if they were involved in something, or if they were guilty, then you really have a major problem, for how will they confess the truth, or how will they aid in getting to it?

By utilizing every possible means—unfortunately!

The problem then is reduced to its essence, which rests upon the following question: how can you distinguish an innocent person from an involved or guilty person? Quickly, quickly, in order not to allow what takes place in secret any chance to persist, or succeed—this then is the first thing that must be taken into consideration, for if what's going on in secret does succeed, a million things will come as a result. The other question, indeed the more difficult and more taxing one, is this: who is innocent?

Let's back off a minute from our personal concerns, in order to see things more clearly. Let's take Israel, for example. Who is an innocent Arab over there after a military attack on an Israeli soldier, or a settler, or any other citizen? All Arabs are Arabs over there, even the ones who collaborate with the Israelis! That's a predicament.

A real predicament.

So when is an innocent person innocent?

If we go back to my personal situation, my problem as I stated before resided in the fact that I, in spite of myself, gave them cause for suspicion. I don't say that out of any special liking for them or desire to defend them, but to point out the predicament that any interested party will surely fall into if they look at the situation impartially and honestly, putting aside personal whims and self-interest.

I repeat: this does not in any way mean that I was guilty. Not at all. I have no idea what happened to that picture, nor is it my style to stir up hatred or start a protest. That's the truth; I'm not lying or trying to disguise the truth. What good would it do me anyway, to lie, or hide things, or try to justify myself, or any such thing after what happened, after suffering that wound that will never heal.

(Really, I hope it will heal.)

(But really, I hope it will heal.)

Lying in such circumstances would be despicable. So what's a little water to a drowning man?

But it doesn't necessarily follow that I was guilty, it just means I couldn't let my anger toward them get the better of me. And so, every time I felt the anger consuming me (yes, honestly, consuming me!) no, devouring me, the way one animal devours another, it would occur to me that such anger was not one hundred percent justifiable, because their suspicions about me began the moment I presented them with a tangible reason for them to be suspicious. It killed me.

My anger with my self at that moment just killed me. Knowing it killed me, especially since I was convinced my "self" was not to blame. Then I would remember that friend of mine who refused to record that name in his address book, out of an intense awareness and sharp perception of the dangers and perils that might come as a result (of writing it down) and I would say how cruel life was! From where had he been blessed with this special quality—this cautiousness—and why hadn't it occurred to me in the least, my whole life, to be cautious about such a thing? Why? And so I would say how unfair life was. It killed me that my anger toward them could not be pure, because of something inside me, because I, because I...

Was my "self" not actually to blame? Was I truly innocent? Hadn't I merely brought upon myself problems that my "self" deserved?

If we take only the visible, tangible actions into consideration, then I am definitely not guilty, in the sense that I certainly did not tear the picture. I did not even touch it, nor did I see anyone else touch it. But...

But, that picture always caught my attention.

The truth is that that picture always caught my attention whenever I passed by it. In fact, it always (I just have to spit it out now) made me upset. Yes. It upset me.

It pissed me off.

Sometimes, well, usually. Okay, I was *always* careful about not looking closely at it. I was afraid my emotions would get the better of me and I would tear it, against my will. You see, as I've said already, I'm always worried my "self" will get me into problems I can't handle. And it always happens.

I really two people?

really two people at least? Maybe more?

And if I am, which one of me is legally, ethically, or morally responsible? And which one is the real me?

I would pass by that picture and rarely look directly at it, out of fear that someone might be watching in order to discern my feelings toward it. Every day I had to pass by it, and many times, because in all simplicity it had been posted on the wall to the right of the entrance of the building I live in, and I usually—and this a natural characteristic I was born with—I usually notice things on the right more than things on the left. It's just the way I am—the way nature intended it to be! There's nothing wrong with my neck, either, or my head, or my eyes, or my ears. That's just the way it is—my attention is naturally drawn to the right for natural, personal reasons I know nothing about. And so, did whoever it was who pasted the picture on that side know me that well? No doubt. Or if not him, whoever sent him to do it. Same difference.

I'm sure it must have been intentional, and that my lot had been drawn. I said chance was to blame, not my "self." I said it from my head and from my heart, and when the mind and the heart join together, conviction is absolute.

Chance!

My lot had been drawn, which explains why they behaved as they did, and their attempts to put an end to the wave of tearings of that picture, that picture in particular out of all the many pictures that were plastered all over the city walls for grand and lofty reasons like martyrdom most of all. But why the campaign over that picture and no other, when there were so many martyrs?

They were given the order—arrest anyone deemed

suspicious, between 8:00 and 9:00 tomorrow morning, in every block of the city. Interrogate them, and detain anyone who confirms your suspicions. And if you can't confirm anything then make an example out of him for the real culprits! (For sure, whoever had done it must have been dangerous and experienced professionals to be able to do what they did, over a period of days, sometimes in broad daylight, without getting caught.)

Whenever I passed by that picture I felt like I was being dared, and when I would try to fathom why, I would get even angrier. That picture was plastered all over the city. The same one, everywhere you went, as if the man never had any other picture taken his whole life. What irritated me most was his smile. I always hate the smile in those pictures, especially the smiles of "important" men. The whole city could be upside down, or total terror could be running rampant through the streets, and meanwhile there they are, smiling (in front of the cameras) to appear "*rassurants*" before the people, to show them that everything was "under control." They were prime examples of "the right man in the right place at the right time." Yes. And the one in the picture was smi...

So does that mean I was actually guilty, and deserved to be punished?

They must have noticed me looking at him (at it—at the picture) in an unusual way (suspicious way)—and it was their duty to notice—and they also must have noticed how my attention was always drawn to the right side. They set out to arrest me, therefore, based on what they observed. And their intention was obvious: make an example out of me. Especially since I deserved it.

I never imagined for a second that my inner disgust for that picture would at some time show on my face or show in my behavior and become obvious to other people—and what other people they turned out to be! Even though I was so careful. I'm careful by nature. I don't remember ever looking directly at that picture, because I never wanted to raise any suspicions. No one knows as well as I do that pictures are under tighter surveillance than all the sensitive and dangerous areas put together, especially that picture, because I understood it to be of intrinsic significance somehow. That's why I always just glimpsed at it. I mean, out of the corner of my eye, sneakily. Sometimes I would be consumed with an intense desire to stare right at it, close up, and take in every detail of it. Until now I didn't really have more than a general idea of what's in that picture. Something incredibly strong and stormy inside me would urge me to look at it long and hard and take in all its details, but I forbid myself from getting too close to it, to avoid the possibility of anyone getting the wrong idea. And I always wondered, especially on those occasions when I was upset about it, that if looking at pictures was grounds for suspicion, then why were they posted on the walls of every street, and every square, and every entrance hall, and every public and private place?

So many parents have gotten dragged by those pictures into problems they never dreamed could happen. Just like that, they would end up paying for their children's "innocent" actions, or maybe reckless or irresponsible actions. But this price they paid—let it be said—was not unfair or tyrannical; it was well-founded. Yes, well-founded. And I say well-founded, and not well-deserved. At any rate, it wasn't unfair or an act of aggression. No little boy ever tore a picture of something his parents considered holy, like a picture of Jesus, for example, or pictures of the saints, or pictures or papers with Quranic verses on them. And no little boy ever tore the picture of a man his parents respected; if it did happen, it was rare—the exception and not the rule. It wasn't unfair, then; things should always be kept in perspective so we don't make a mountain out of a molehill, or grapes out of figs, and mix everything up.

It is so difficult for an innocent person to take a good, close look at his innocence, or to see it objectively; to look at it antagonistically would be simply impossible. But this is wrong. Totally wrong. The right thing to do is to look at one's innocence objectively at least. At least. Or through the eyes of the adversary, or the eyes of the enemy. Yes! The eyes of the enemy! Otherwise, the person will remain forever vulnerable to situations like mine.

(And then the person would deserve it!)

I don't think anyone knows my *self* as well as I do. That's why I say what I say. I know more about my self than my self does, which is why I am so afraid of it; that's a fact. In his book, *The Secret Life of Salvador Dali*, Salvador Dali, who is both narrator and author, tells about not knowing how certain emotions of his evolved as they did, leading him to behave in surprising and unexpected ways. He gives several examples of such incidents, one of which was once, when he was very, very young, he was walking over a bridge with a little friend of his. Suddenly, he pushed his friend off the highest point of the bridge, several meters up, causing him multiple fractures. His friend nearly died. Another time, suddenly everyone—family and guests—rushed outside to look at an airplane up in the sky, and at one point while running behind them he looked back and saw his

[handwritten margin note: why Dali?]

baby sister crawling to catch up with everyone. So he turned around and kicked her (in the eye, if I remember correctly). When I read those stories I was really frightened; my heart pounded. I felt certain that if he were to go on, eventually he would get to some story of mine. In particular, the story of the time I shot my hunting rifle at a friend and buddy of mine—not to kill him out of jealousy or hatred or anything, but just to shoot at him and kill him, without any motivation or desire to destroy him. Just like that... to kill, not to hurt. The judge tried very hard to understand everything I said, but what I said had been in response to questions that didn't mean anything to me; they seemed irrelevant, and totally beside the point. I knew what they expected to hear, so I gave them exactly what they wanted.

"Did you shoot at him?"

"Yes."

"Weren't you afraid you might kill him?"

"It didn't occur to me that I might kill him."

"Why did you shoot at him?"

"..." Silence. ⟵

I was seven years old. My friend and I were on a hunting trip with our fathers. When we stopped to rest, I saw my friend heading off somewhere (later I found out where.) Suddenly, I grabbed my father's rifle while he wasn't looking—I almost say while I wasn't looking, because it was not something I consciously decided or did willfully. I aimed the rifle right at him, fired, and hit him. Fortunately for me, (and for him of course! Excuse me!) I didn't kill him. It was a serious wound, but nothing more than that. It wasn't life threatening, nor did it pose any danger to any part of him. It merely left a surface scar on his neck and ear (until today). Nevertheless, the matter ended up in court, against the wishes of our fathers who, out of civility—

especially his father—turned the incident into an opportunity to show the depth and strength of the friendship that existed between them and consequently between our families.

"The important thing is that no one died, and no one was permanently injured."

Everyone repeated that, and whenever I heard it I felt at ease, mostly because it conveyed to me his or her sense of ease. However, deep down I didn't agree with it. Why was the absence of death "the important thing" and not death? I mean, not dying is not so unusual; every day, no, every hour and every second not dying "happens." (That's how I used to think at that age; even in my early youth I had a contemplative, philosophical bent.)

"Why did you fire at him?"

"..." Silence! Silence! ⟵

Whenever I fell silent, the judge felt sorry for me, and gave me the feeling he wanted to hug me to his chest and kiss me. I don't know why my silence elicited in him such noble feelings toward me. With my father, though, one time, when he pushed the question, I answered. I told him I hadn't expected the bullet to reach him. I thought he was too far away to hit him. I told him, "Actually, what I meant to do was, after shooting at him, say something like, 'Scared you, didn't I!'" I said I felt very bad that I never got to say it. That's what I told my father, which is something you can't really reply to, because it seems profound, or because it was profound, although not everything that is profound is true.

Up until very recently I have always been afraid that I might push a friend walking down the street beside me into a speeding car, so I would always switch places with him and make sure he was on the side next to the wall, in a place safe from any random, involuntary action of mine.

People bring problems onto themselves. This is my motto from which I take counsel in such situations.

I know oh so well that it is difficult to live this way, spending all our time flagellating ourselves, since it makes it impossible to be vehemently and purely angry at the oppressor (oppressor between quotations), especially when we are the ones being oppressed. I know! But to what extent is this oppressor really an oppressor when he asks you about a person whose name you wrote with your own hand into your own address book, along with his phone number—the correct number at that—and asks you where you met him and on what occasion, and you tell him, "I don't know." Is he crazy enough to believe that?

Well, yes, it *might* be the truth, but it is less likely in the eyes of an interrogator, especially the kind before whom I stood. And let's not forget the word *might*.

Might and nothing more.

It *might* be the truth.

How can an interrogator, who is unlike other interrogators — because his neck is also on the line—be expected to think I truly just forgot, when it (only *might*) be true? That's why I think that maybe life is the true oppressor, and chance the murderer.

Yes, murderer! Because what happened to me is no sweet story that brings bellyfuls of laughter to those who hear it, or helps them sleep well at night. I already mentioned how the doctor's wife ended her story in the Robert Altman film, *Short Cuts*, by assuring him that her partner that day in the car didn't come inside her.

As for me, I ended up with a new name. They gave it to me to replace the name my parents chose for me, the name I have always been called, affectionately, for so many years, the name my friends have called me millions of times, the name acquaintances have called me, and close friends, and my sisters, and brothers, my wife, my son.

(Did they really have to do that? I don't think so.)

Oh, yes, they made sure to call me my new name in my own house, after they led me there so my wife and I could make coffee for them and we could finish our conversation, with my son sitting next to me (not in my lap) because they...

My son was sitting next to me for a reason. When he rushed toward me after I opened the door (they didn't allow me to ring the doorbell and signal my wife, the way we usually do when I come home with unexpected visitors. They didn't allow me so she wouldn't be able to take precautions and hide things they didn't want her to hide, or maybe they didn't allow me to ring in order to put pressure on me—they wanted to surprise her and catch her in some indecent or compromising position. Or maybe, and most logically, it was for both reasons.) So, when my son rushed toward me, after hearing the door open, they yelled at him, "Get back!"

And I wanted him to not come close. I wanted him to stay back, so he would not witness (in such close proximity) those ugly moments. Probably the ugliest possible moments in the world are when a father is humiliated in front of his son. When I used to hear stories about fathers subjected to that kind of treatment, by armed men at military checkpoints on the road, for example, or in their homes, inside their own houses, or other various places, I really ached inside. I remember someone telling me once what happened to him at one of the checkpoints. He said the soldier slapped him in front of his son, because he hadn't stopped the car right where the soldier was standing. He had gone just a bit too far, forcing the soldier to have to take a step or two. The soldier ordered him to get out of the car, and when he stood before him, the soldier slapped him hard, causing the cigarette he was smoking to fall from his hand (the soldier's hand). So he ordered him to bend down and pick it up. He had to obey. During the whole ordeal he did not look at his son once, nor did he look at him for several days afterwards. This story pained me, as do all such stories; but, they remained just that: other people's stories. How quickly we forget these stories… until they happen to us, and then we go wild.

I wished and hoped with everything within me that my son would not be there, that he would be, for example, with… with whom? In all the time since he was born he never once spent the night away from home. In the evening his mother takes care of him and gives him his bottle after he has his bath and gets into his pajamas. He still drinks a bottle once a day, only in the evening, which does not bother us at all, his mother and me. Actually, we like it, and all three of us take pleasure in those moments. My favorite time of the day is the evening, when he comes running to me with cries of joy as I open the door. "Baba! Baba!" He hears me the moment my feet shuffle up the stairs. He cocks his ears and then, when he hears the key turning in the lock, he rushes to the door. No sooner does the door open than there he is.

"Get back!"

The boy didn't understand what he was hearing; he continued in his rush toward the door still singing, "Baba! Baba!"

Up until that point… up until the moment I entered the house, and despite everything, despite the many harsh and difficult moments I lived through, I hadn't shed a single tear.

But there, there in my home, unfortunately (I say unfortunately because it was the most inappropriate place possible) the tears flowed in spite of me. They burst forth all on their own, as if they were a separate being; they flowed down my cheeks, and kept flowing. I was completely incapable of doing anything to stop them. Never in my life had I experienced such a mixture of strong, contradictory, varied, and unsteady emotions, which were primarily feelings of shame and embarrassment, probably the most difficult for me to bear. Shame and embarrassment before my son!

No! That was more than I could bear.

When my son approached me, one of them pushed him back with his hand to stop him from reaching me, but he wouldn't be stopped. And so he pushed him hard, causing him to fall onto the bare floor—the entranceway to our house is not carpeted. Fortunately, he landed on his bottom, which was padded by his thick diaper, and so he wasn't hurt. Nevertheless he started to cry and was clearly bewildered and surprised by all kinds of emotions that are so confusing a person doesn't even know what to call them, because they don't even have names. As for his mother, my wife, she took a long time to appear. I was sure she would appear, even though I hoped she wouldn't, but she was taking a long time, and still she hadn't appeared.

Okay. My wife didn't come even though I expected her to.

I was expecting her to greet me before my son, because I was later than usual getting home. So wasn't she worried? I thought she would keep the boy safely away, after quickly realizing that the situation was not normal—take him to the bedroom, give him his toys, and close the door. She knew better than anyone the kinds of things that go on around here; her street smarts were as good as anyone else's who lives around here. She knew what kinds of things might happen, so what had changed? The matter really shocked me! Which was the last thing I needed. What had been going on in my house in my absence? All kinds of ideas came into my mind. One thing and then its complete opposite would occur to me mere seconds apart. Then all these thoughts spun around and got all mixed up, turning my brain into a kind of primordial matter, or chaos, or vacuum… I think I fainted at that point, because I don't remember anything after that except sitting on a chair in the kitchen, my son on another chair nearby, sitting up like an adult, not moving a muscle.

Yes. Yes. Later on, some time after that, I got the courage to ask my son about what happened while I was unconscious, and he answered me.

"Uncle went 'peepee!'"

Was that possible? I asked him while his mother was not around; and I was able to understand everything. It seems they had the "key" and knew well how to use it, even in front of my son. In his presence! They succeeded in bringing me back to consciousness very quickly indeed, and without having to administer any first aid, which they probably didn't know anything about anyway.

My wife did not witness that scene; I am totally and completely sure of that. I'm no child who thinks that everything he hopes to be true really is true, nor am I the kind of person to get lost in illusions. Furthermore, I don't base my conviction on the fact that she told me she didn't see me come in, but rather I base it on what I saw for myself: she did not appear until later, a long time after we had gone into the kitchen, and when she did come into the kitchen I immediately noticed her reaction to seeing me. I say I noticed her reaction even though I wasn't really seeing clearly. My eyes were clouded, but I was able to see with my other senses, unmistakably. Yes, I saw her, and I saw her reaction, which was the reaction of someone seeing for the first time, not the second time. This is an indisputable fact in my mind, with no room for doubt whatsoever.

We were six at dinner: us—myself, my wife and my son—and them. There were three of them. In the kitchen, which is also our dining room. My wife, as usual, was serving.

"I like a woman to be a good housewife and a respectable woman at the same time," said the one who had questioned me at the beginning of my whole ordeal, and the one who apparently didn't like the food my wife served him. She didn't respond.

"Is this how you honor your guests?" the second one said, meaning he also didn't like the food. My wife had fried some eggs and opened a can of sardines; in other words, she served what was available, because first of all, she did not really want to honor them, and second, they forbade her from leaving the house or using the phone or answering it either. Whenever the phone did ring, and it rang several times—after all, evening is the time when the phone rings most—our son would break his silence and say to his mother, "Mama. Telephone." Then one of them would shut him up, either by shouting at him or by poking him if that didn't work, and he would slip back into his silence all over again.

"I'm not eating this," the third one said. "For such a delicious woman, your food sure leaves a lot to be desired. I like you better."

I heard for myself what that last one said. I heard it with my own two ears that were still as yet unharmed. When I heard it, I slipped into oblivion; I vanished. I did not look at her, out of shame, and because I wouldn't be able to control myself if she were to look at me. I don't even know if she did look at me. I have no idea. I never asked her about it afterwards, nor did she ask me.

When she had first come in, her hair was a mess, and so was her blouse, no all her clothes, as if she had been in a fight. But she…

But, oh gods of the earth, and oh evil demons! She was alone when she came in to where we were, and the three of them who came there with me hadn't left me alone for a second. I had not been unconscious for more than a few seconds, a few minutes at the very worst, so what had happened?

"There is a limit to everything," I said, but it was as though I were talking to myself. I said it with my eyes glued to the plate in front of me, and I stayed that way for several moments, not lifting my eyes, afraid of what I might see. I could feel all of them smiling. Then, one of them said to another while looking at me for sure, "If only he would speak when he is supposed to."

Then the three of them refused to eat, insisting the "meal" was unfit for them (not our quality!), insisting the "meal" might be good enough for the family, but it wasn't at all fit for them (not up to our standards!). My wife can be hot-tempered sometimes; she can't always control her reactions. That's why I constantly worried she would come out and shock them with some kind of sharp response. It wasn't that I didn't think they deserved it; on the contrary, they more than deserved it. I was worried they would retaliate with "equal measure." I was afraid she might say something like, we were working people who had to get up early in the morning and therefore weren't free to stay up all hours of the night, to which they would respond that they, too, were working people, otherwise they wouldn't have to be there in the first place.

"Bitch, do you think we enjoy your company so much?"

"Mnnhnhlbm," I mumbled, producing sounds I myself did not recognize, my eyes constantly on my plate, which was still empty.

"What's wrong with the jackass now?" one of them asked, trying to figure out what I had said.

"It's your father who's a jackass!" my wife retorted from where she was at the sink. Then she added, "Go eat at your own houses!"

Sudden silence. The kind of silence before someone aims to shoot. Shoot at whom? When? In that moment my son started to cry, so the one next to him gave him a slap. My wife threw the plate she was holding at him, which just missed hitting him in the head. If only he hadn't been so close to our son, I'm sure she would have hit him, but she had been careful not to hit the boy. The plate smashed against the wall. The man got up with measured calm and went toward her. When she saw him coming she backed away, so he rushed at her, grabbed her by the hair, and dragged her into an inside room, while she struggled to get away from him, screaming and cursing him the whole time. He said only one thing to her throughout all of that—I mean throughout the part we saw; and he said it with the quiet, mournful demeanor of someone who has been slighted in some way. He said, "You broke your promise, you whore!" After that I didn't hear anything except my son's crying and wailing. At one point I looked over at him, after the battle in the kitchen moved into the other room, and I tried to pick him up in order to quiet him down and comfort him. But one of them took him from me and plopped him back down into his chair like a sack of potatoes. Then he yelled, in a sharp tone I hadn't heard from him earlier, or from any of the others (so was he the boss?). He said the child must go to sleep immediately, because tonight there was a lot of work to be done. A few minutes later the one who dragged my wife inside came back, with her, and said, "Go on! Hurry up! Put him to sleep." But how? How were we supposed to put him to sleep so fast? The matter was out of our hands. He needed time to fall asleep, and he hadn't had his bottle yet, either.

"Now!" he repeated—but not the same one—the one who seemed to be the boss.

So his mother picked him up and carried him to the bedroom. The same one followed her to help, as he said loud enough for all to hear, "I'll come and help you."

However, out in the kitchen we kept hearing noises from the bedroom indicating he hadn't fallen asleep yet. So one of them said to me, "You know, you're an ass!" I honestly did not understand why he said that, especially since I thought that if anything, he should go on about the strange sounds I had made a bit earlier. Then he said, "Don't you have some sleeping pills or something?"

Only then did I understand.

But all we had were adult-strength sleeping pills, not for children; we'd never needed anything like that to get our son to sleep. Would it be all right to give them to a child? "Give him half of one," he said, and then he yelled loud enough for my wife to hear him from the bedroom, calling her by her son's name—with all due respect—to come speak to me, "Come talk to your husband, Imm*..." (It wouldn't be right for me to reveal

---

* Lit. "Mother of." Arab women are commonly and politely addressed as "Mother of (first-born son)."

my son's name here; his friends would recognize who he was.)

Indeed, he himself might find out one day that I was talking about him. That's why I have to avoid mentioning it. You see, my son is still very young and won't remember any of it; he'll forget, and we will help him forget, his mother and I. I, especially.

(I, for sure.)

My wife came out, accompanied by the one who went to help her, holding the boy close to her chest. She looked at everyone but me. The one who had called her said, "Your husband wants you." So I told her to give him a quarter of a sleeping pill from the bottle in the drawer next to the bed.

"You jackass!" said the one who was always saying that. Then he said, addressing my wife, "God help you with him! No doubt you'll have a nice spot in heaven for all you've had to put up with!"

Then he said, "Half!"

Addressing me now he continued, "Jackass!"

My wife went right away, without a word, not accepting, nor refusing, nor resisting, just went to the bedroom, returned moments later without the boy, filled a glass with water, disappeared again, and then within minutes we didn't hear another sound.

"Whew," one of them sighed, echoed in turn by his buddies.

All I cared about in those moments was my son. Did the dose kill him? Wasn't it too much? Didn't his mother give him a little less than half? She could have, after all, since she was all alone; no one followed her. I wished I could say something that would get me some reassurance from her, like, "I notice he went right to sleep," and she would say, "A tiny amount of those sleeping pills is plenty for such a young child to sleep, especially one like our son who is not used to them, making them especially quick and effective." But such a sneaky, coded conversation between us then was impossible. They would certainly figure it out and use it as an excuse to accuse us, or insult us, me especially. That's even if they allowed it in the first place.

"Well?" the one who had called her said. "Are you still hungry, or are you full from just looking at the food? Personally, I'm still hungry," he added, "and I can't sleep on an empty stomach. I won't be able to sleep a wink."

So the honored dinner guest was going to sleep over!

Dinner would not be the end of it. We were going to spend the entire night, and what a long night it was going to be. Were his buddies going to stay too? But we didn't have enough room for all of them, unless they each wanted to choose a spot to sleep in; unless one of them... we'll see.

"You will not die until your hour has come." I said to myself.

"Well?" the one who had gone inside with her said.

The whole time after coming back from putting our son to sleep (or drugging him, that is) my wife washed the dishes mechanically and nervously, and didn't answer any of their questions.

"Well?" the third one said—the one who was now patting me on the shoulder. He said it demandingly and assertively, to impress upon us—on me and my wife—that the situation now called for an answer, or a reaction, or a response, or something other than silence.

"This isn't a restaurant," my wife fired at them in all conciseness, economy, frankness, and sharpness. One single, sufficient shot that needed no repetition whatsoever.

So what was my wife planning, exactly? What did she have in mind that made her decide to push things toward a dead end? Toward a lost cause? Did she know something I didn't know? Had she managed to figure out something I couldn't? Or what?

Why didn't she—as far as dinner was concerned—show them some good intentions and say to them, for example, as a kind of apology, that this was all we had that night. She hadn't been expecting anyone, so she wasn't prepared, but if they liked, she would be happy to go down to the store before it closed and buy what she could to prepare a decent meal.

Really, my wife should have understood that they hadn't come to eat, but rather to see, and hear, and know, and get to the bottom of things—which would be accomplished—in their opinion—in the manner in which they were proceeding. Also, to guarantee success—again in their opinion—a certain level of provocation was required in order to catch the one being provoked off guard and make him divulge things he would never divulge if calm and collected. We might not condone this kind of logic, not wanting to be its victims, but nevertheless it was something they could easily defend. So let them go ahead and do it if they wanted; we couldn't change it, nor could they. Let's just continue to show them our good intentions and our sincere desire to have the truth they wanted revealed be revealed. How could my wife go against this indisputable logic? Or was I the one whose ability to understand and perceive had become ineffective, along with my ability to figure things out?

What did she have in mind?

Unless she was thinking that in any event, and no matter how nice we were to them, they were going to hurt us anyway, so we should hurt them as much as we could. If that was the case, I think she was totally wrong. It would also mean that not only was she completely disregarding the particular situation we were in there in our house, but in the entire country; or it would mean she was completely unaware of it, which was more likely because she never followed the news at all—not in the papers, or magazines, or on the radio or television, not even in conversations with people. There was nothing she hated more than talking about politics. If only I could explain it to her. Right then. If they would just let me take her aside for a couple of minutes to explain the situation to her, to tell her that because of the general situation in the country now these kinds of things can happen. Even if we were good people who didn't support or condone such things, we just had to let the storm rip through without letting it uproot us. Take them in as guests. Play their game. They called themselves guests; so be it. Sometimes you just have to. Let's treat them like guests; maybe they will behave like guests. Let's try every possible way out and not miss any opportunity. Let's not give up hope. Let's not push things to a confrontation that will mean suicide for us. Because, my dear wife, I don't know why you think you are going to win, and against whom? Against them? They're just tools. I mean, they're simply following orders. As for winning against the others, they have no idea what is happening to you right now. And if you're trying to charge them with something, like making them feel guilty over your suicide or something, well they won't even hear about it. Even if people like you hear about you, they won't understand your death the way you intended it. And nothing could be simpler than proving what I'm saying is right: have you ever heard of anyone doing what you're thinking of doing now? Don't you know you're not the first person to get into a mess like this, and you won't be the last? Have some sense!

The most important gift nature has bestowed upon human beings is the brain. It distinguishes us above all matter, plants, and animals. With it we are special. So let's use it. Use it, my darling wife, mother of my child. I order you!

"Make them whatever they want."

This command slipped out of my mouth from nowhere. I waited. I waited for her to say, "As you wish," and show them how much she respected me; to be generous and show them how obedient she was; to show them how dear I was to her, to her heart—so dear she couldn't possibly deny me any request. I had given her a rare opportunity to show me her love and respect, and right in the middle of those extremely tense moments, by far the tensest one could possibly imagine. Such moments—if they happen at all—don't come along more than once in a lifetime; they are too momentous to happen more than once. I had given her a rare opportunity to show me love, love I needed desperately at that moment, as desperately as a drowning man needs air. In so many words I had said to her, "Save me! I'm drowning!"

More than giving her a rare opportunity, I was offering her a clever way out of having refused to make them a decent meal, and without even appearing to be backing down. I had cleared the way for her to back down as a winner, on top, in that even though she had dared to refuse to follow their orders, she was prepared to rectify things on the basis of her husband's request. But she was stubborn, hard-headed, and unable to comprehend any of the dangers I tried to make known to her by giving that command, which slipped out of me of its own accord—that's true—but which, after thinking about it deeply and with complete detachment—had been entirely appropriate, as if, in view of how appropriate it really was, it had come as the result of careful planning.

I waited for her to respond in the way I expected, but she just went on silently busying her hands and herself with the dirty dishes in the sink.

"Didn't you hear me?" I said in case she hadn't gotten it the first time, hoping she would get it the second time and do what I was urging her to do; come to my aid, for I was done for. Certainly she was aware of that and no one needed to explain it to her.

I was done for.

She knew they were set on humiliating me in front of her; that was what she was actually witnessing with her own two eyes. They wanted to force out of me the information they thought I had. So what she should do was show them clearly that no matter what they did, they could never succeed in demeaning me in her eyes. I would always be her husband, her crown of glory, the father of her son and all future children, and no power on earth was capable of lowering her high esteem for me even one iota.

O cross of my salvation! O dear wife! Come on!

"Why don't *you* do it? *You* get up and make them whatever they want!"

No!

I was expecting anything but this response from my wife, and in front of them, no less. Never, ever, from the moment I met her and all during our married life had she ever said anything like that to me. She knew how much I loved her and respected her and how polite and kind I always was to her, so what had happened? What had brought this on?

I expected anything but for this lethal blow to come from there, from that direction, from my last available refuge—my wife, the pillow upon which I rest my head of all its trouble and pains, my life companion in sickness and in health, for better or for worse, the mother of my child, the woman who gave him birth and suckled him, the keeper of all my secrets, my mate in body and soul. When I get little pimples or infected hair follicles on my body, my wife likes to pop them with a needle and pluck out the hair trapped inside. She does it so carefully, lovingly, and patiently. I love that. I love... I surrender to her and to the touch of her fingers all over my back and the delicate poke of the needle into my skin.

Could this be possible?

I expected everything but this from her. Not this destructive response. I tried to get up from my chair right away, the moment I heard it, because hesitation in such critical situations is danger itself. The only thing that might be worse would be total surrender. That was my first attempt at standing up since being forced to sit down and ordered not to move. But just as I was about to succeed in standing up I found myself sitting back down all over again. So I tried again, but some force kept pulling me back down. Then I realized it was the one sitting beside me who was pulling me down every time my rear end lifted out of the chair. Then, at one point during my repeated attempts to stand up, I grabbed a fork that was there in front of me and threw it at my wife. It hit her just above the eye, just missing it, and made her shriek in pain. The one who had called to her looked over at me and said, "You're really something! You dare to throw a fork at your wife without giving a damn where it might hit her. And I thought you were polite and peaceful, but it seems you can be violent when you want to be. A snake in the grass."

I don't know where I got the strength to throw the fork far enough and hard enough to hurt her with it, when my hand was practically paralyzed.

Then the one who had dragged her inside earlier got up to try to comfort her, but she squirmed free of him and backed away, hiding her face in her hands, and started to cry. But he persisted and kept trying to pull her hands away from her face.

"How have you managed to live with him for so long, the animal?"

She didn't say anything back. She didn't say, for example, "He's my husband, not an animal," adding another venomous, defiant response to her list while she was still at it. It was at this point that I noticed that she was not defending me one bit with her responses. She was defending only herself, or at best, her son. But not me at all.

"If only you knew how sweet living with her is!" I said.

Yes!

Yes, I actually said, "If only you knew…"

I heard myself saying it, word by word, and even though I didn't plan to say it, what I meant by it was something I realized later, which was to make them think I thought she was a bad wife. But strangely enough, it did not elicit the slightest reaction from her or any of them either. Strange.

I expected what I said would encourage them to step in on my wife's behalf. As I was saying it I imagined—although I didn't want it to be true—that I was playing right into their hands. My being rude to my wife made them look better. The fact that they acted as though they hadn't heard anything, or noticed anything, really surprised me. They behaved like perfect guests. Guests who did not want to take any notice of a disagreement between a husband and his wife. It was as if nothing happened at all.

"Are we going to eat tonight, or what?" said the one who had called her by our son's name earlier, since the one who had been trying to console her came back to the table. She just kept crying and covering her face with her hands.

"Quit that now," continued the one in charge. "You can work things out with hubby later. Now we have serious work to do." Then he added, "But first we must eat. Immediately!"

"We must eat immediately!" he shouted, as he got up from his seat, headed directly for my wife, dragged her by the hair over to me, and smashed our heads together.

"Patch things up some other time when we're not around!"

I was dizzy. My head was spinning; everything was spinning. Not until later, a while later, was I able to get back to normal, after seeing my wife at the sink… yes, at the sink.

Then, and only then, did my honorable wife go to the sink to prepare them a good meal.

Then, and only then, did my honorable wife understand what she had to do. I was furious with her! She slaughtered me; she delivered the final blow.

No! Not from you my darling wife, my life companion, my partner for better or for worse, not from you the deadly blow. Why hadn't you understood me? Why hadn't you decoded my message to you? It was no command I had given you; I had addressed you graciously, like one gracious person to another. Why did you give them room to step in between us?

Come to think of it from the time I had come home she didn't try even once to approach me and see what had happened to me. If her excuse for that was that she knew they wouldn't let her if she tried, well at least she should have tried anyway. I wouldn't have blamed her for failing. But let's say, for the sake of argument, that it really had been a valid reason, well then why didn't she look over at the wounds all over my body, even once? A fleeting glance would have been enough to comfort me.

But she did not look at me at all, as if I were the plague!

"The wife is the husband's enemy." I said, and everyone heard me. Indeed, I had said it so they would.

"Let her fix the meal!"

How strange. How crazy! How could they not care about our bickering when every point of weakness from us could bring them closer to their goal? That was really astonishing. How…?

So I shut up.

Spaghetti. Quick, easy, decent. They liked it, with salad, eggs, sardines. A great meal. We sat and ate.

She was next to him, the one who seemed to be in charge, and she was more than happy about it. And the fact she was forced to sit there doesn't change my judgment against her one bit; she was totally content now to be sitting there. She didn't squirm, for example, as she might if she had sat down beside a snake, or as if her heart were filled with anxiety, anger, hatred, or some such emotion.

Then—she filled his plate first, although she really wasn't under any pressure to. He thanked her with sincere politeness and she nearly thanked him back. Then she sat down next to him, even though she didn't have to. She chose to sit next to him and she did it without any shyness or shame. And I saw him as best I could with my eyes in that condition reach over and place his hand on her thigh with total calm. She didn't move or jerk back in fright or disgust. No, she didn't flinch. Not even out of modesty.

She smiled; she nearly laughed when he joked, "What is the epitome of laziness?"

He looked directly at the faces of everyone present, especially hers, which showed how diligently she was trying to figure out the answer to the question. When no one answered, he was very pleased and said, "Give up?" Then he turned to her and said, "Even you?"

She nearly said yes. He was overjoyed when it became clear that none of us (my wife and I at least) knew the answer.

"For a man to marry a pregnant woman!" he finally said.

She nearly smiled. Yes. As for me, I laughed; yes, I laughed openly. I had to. Let's not forget I was the one all this was directed at. Furthermore, it was my house and I was responsible for everything that went on inside it. I was "the man of the house," and in that capacity it was my responsibility to laugh at a joke told by one of my guests, especially when it was a good one, circumstances aside, and even if he had been using it to look "cute" in front of my wife.

Oh, if only the matter ended there with that joke! But jokes on such topics and in such circumstances can only prepare the way for taking graver steps, which is why I was not at all surprised when, as soon as the laughter died down, the boss proceeded to ask her if she was pregnant.

"Are you expecting?" he asked (and actually he was being very polite in choosing this word "expecting," which sounds much more respectable than "pregnant.")

My wife hesitated before answering. Yes, she answered him! "I think so."

Oh my God. Oh my God! No, no, no. That was an extremely, extremely dangerous answer. Didn't she realize that? Was it possible that she did not realize she was thereby inviting him and all of them into our intimate matters?

"You think so? You mean, you're not sure? You mean, you're still in the process of trying?"

Exactly! He hit it right on the mark. We were still trying and

103

weren't yet sure if she had conceived. At that time we were still trying. Yes, trying. And we assumed we would succeed, because when we had tried for our first baby, it had been easy. There had been no problem.

My wife did not answer his last question. (Out of embarrassment? Around whom? Me?) She kept her eyes focused on something on the table in front of her. His hand kept realighting on her thigh.

"Doesn't it bother you your husband is so lazy and wastes so much time?"

The boss was still making his advance into the world my wife had opened up to him when with a faint but profound smile she answered, "No."

Yes, good job, dear wife, but go on. Tell them quickly why not. But they didn't allow her to do that—they burst out laughing and kept at it a long time. She waited for them to stop so she could clarify what she meant by "No." But then when they settled down, she didn't talk. She just kept silent, as if "No" was all she intended to say. But how? How could she just say "No" without clarifying herself, knowing well they would understand it the way they wanted and not the way she wanted. They would interpret it as meaning my wife thought I was lazy but it didn't bother her, because it gave her an excuse to remedy the situation with some other man, or other men. Therefore, they had the right to strive to be among those men. So come on, dear wife, go on, complete your sentence, and tell them what you mean is that my laziness doesn't bother you because I am not lazy. Go on, continue. Say, "No, he's not lazy." Control the damage. Control encouraging them toward the source of all our secrets. Their attempts to infiltrate us are destroyed each time we join together… unless… unless you've got it all figured out and you think collaborating is somehow going to be the way out of this crisis, so you decided to collaborate at your husband's expense. But, dear wife, if this is the plan that came to your mind, and you're convinced of it, then I insist you are wrong. There's only one possibility by which you would not be wrong, which is if that's what you actually want—to confirm that your husband is lazy, in which case you might as well just make an open invitation: Come and get me, boys!

"Would you like some help?" the boss asked. To tell the truth, he was a handsome young man. Classy.

Message received!

Message received, loud and clear, no doubt about it, and no need to explain. He understood what my wife meant. His question—offering to help—was based on that understanding. She kept quiet, not answering no matter how many times he repeated the question. So what was all the silence supposed to mean? Yes or no? Why not just answer frankly and firmly? She had obviously proven she was capable of that!

This is when I said to myself, now is the right time to ask permission to get up and go to the sink. They appeared to be in a calm mood, and surely they wanted to give some proof to my wife they were good-natured and well-intentioned. And besides, they could see with their own eyes I couldn't eat and I really, really needed some water. (It had become clear they weren't intending to kill me; if they had wanted to do that they would have. Really, from the very start that morning while I was in their "custody" the only thing dictating what they should do was their own wishes and their own assumptions.) Certainly they would permit me to get up for one second to go to the sink to drink or something else like that.

The big knife over there near the sink. I could see its sharp blade shining all the way from where I was at the table. I felt I had enough strength to do what could no longer be avoided, quickly and effectively. Fast.

"Well?"

Oh God! I wished I had asked to go to the sink before he called us "back to work." If only he had been one minute behind me. But I shouldn't lose hope. I had to try, despite knowing how difficult it would be for him to grant such a request during work time. (Something unbelievable about that man—work time was sacred to him, pure prayer. He wouldn't even breathe if breathing didn't have some purpose, nor would he let anyone else breathe except to support work efforts. And even more than that, nearing absolute perfection, he didn't make mistakes.) And so, despite knowing how difficult it would be for him to grant such a request, I decided to try anyway. What would I lose? And those favorable conditions I already mentioned encouraged me—they all appeared to be in a good mood, especially him.

With remarkably sincere politeness completely devoid of any sarcasm, he addressed my wife. "Would you mind if we had some coffee?"

It was going to be a long night, and there was a lot of work to be done. The evening was still young. Yes, the perfect time for coffee. And despite the good mood I had enjoyed so far, I was beginning to get fed up.

("Excuse me!")

A strong, strange feeling was welling up inside me, issuing forth from long ago and far away.

The truth is I had started to sense this feeling getting stronger and stronger from the moment I came home and saw my son running toward me... How had they known where my house was? How did they find it without any hesitation? Without asking anybody! They stopped right at the entrance to the building, went directly to the right floor, proceeded right to the apartment, without seeking any guidance from me. And then, when we got to the door, they gave me the right key from among the chain of keys I had been carrying, then somehow lost, and which eventually ended up in their possession. But before I put the key into the lock, I reached up to ring the doorbell—to ring it and alert my wife of unexpected guests—but they stopped me, pushing my hand from the doorbell to the lock. My wife did not greet me at the door. So, had she had prior knowledge of my coming home with them? Had she been informed?

"I want some coffee, too."

This voice came from inside the house, and it came with the surprising suddenness of a gunshot, for it was a voice I recognized. It was that of the fourth man at the office. Had he been at the house a long time, or had he just arrived? Had he gotten there before us? Had he been with my wife in the room (bedroom or living room?) preventing her from greeting me at the door, in order to pressure me into giving in and divulging secrets? When they dragged her by her hair... had they dragged her in to him? Was he...?

"In bed!"

The boss had asked him if he wanted to drink the coffee in bed. So what was he doing there on the bed? What was going on? What kind of additional pressure was this intended to inflict on me?

I had been waiting for the answer. Indeed, I really wanted to know the answer. I mean, I really wanted to know where he wanted to drink his coffee. When he hesitated, I wanted to ask (for myself) but I changed my mind, not wanting to hear an answer I couldn't bear. My ability to bear with things was beginning to weaken. Even worse, something occurred to me: a notion was taking hold of me, a feeling, that I was about to divulge something!

"Did you want to say something?" the boss asked me.

Strange. As if he saw me begin to say something and then stop. No doubt my desire to speak showed on my face, strong as it was.

"How would you like it?" my wife asked, getting up from the chair beside him.

"You'll have to excuse us and be patient with us tonight, but every extra minute is his fault." He (the boss) pointed his finger at me.

"Make yourselves at home. Take your time and do your work. It's your duty," my wife said.

Could it be? Had she finally understood things as I was hoping, and started behaving accordingly? Had she figured out that this calm, polite style would force them to be calm and polite too? Had she finally been convinced the only way we could convince them I was innocent was to open up everything to them—our hearts, our minds, and the contents of our house. Great! This was a very positive step. Refreshing. One more bit of proof that with intuition and instincts a woman can sense everything. No need for volumes of words for her to grasp things. Women are clever by nature, but her position (my wife's, that is) from this point forward was going to be difficult and delicate, for the difference between being easy-going and easy-to-get was not clearly defined with respect to our visitors. Niceness may well be taken as easiness and lead us into a mess we could certainly do without. I couldn't anymore. And speaking of that…

108

Speaking of that, who told her what happened? How did she find out I was under investigation, that I had been accused of tearing the picture, or of hiding information about whomever tore it, or of being party to something or connected to something they were privy to but we weren't. Who told her all that?

Anyway, this was not the problem now. The problem now was trust: their trust in me. That was the key to everything. Therefore, if my wife succeeded in helping me gain their trust, we would arrive at the solution, come into safe waters, as they say. That was our dream, our goal, our desire. That was why my wife had to behave with utmost cleverness and use everything within her power—so we could reach what we were hoping for. And it was not only in our interest, but in theirs, too. After all, they were people, just like us, no matter how evil they were, or rather, no matter how evil they seemed to be. They were simply under obligation to reach a goal, a goal they must reach in order to satisfy their superiors. No, their conscience. If their actions showed a certain amount of harshness, well that was only because they believed the only thing preventing them from succeeding in getting what they wanted was my refusing to talk. And that was why it was so necessary for my wife to help me now—so we could be saved—to act smart, smart, smart, and wise too, and know any mistake now would be unacceptable and inexcusable. A person really should catch on quickly, especially in a situation like this, which does not allow for repeated mistakes, indeed in which a mistake could be fatal. Wisdom dictated that she be extremely careful not to give them the slightest reason to confuse being nice with being easy. At any rate, there was no cause for concern in this regard, for she was her parents' daughter, the daughter of a family fortified by hundreds of years of uprightness, true faith, and piety. Even more than hundreds of years. No one has ever heard of one girl or one woman in that family to have gone astray—God forbid! Or that she disobeyed her husband in any way. Nor had there been a single soul who did not recommend her to me or encourage me to marry her. No, not even one. And never was there a day in which I left my home or returned to my home and had any doubt about her, or even the shadow of a doubt, or misgiving of any kind. I always left home with ease and peace of mind and returned equally at ease. Now, too, there was no cause for worry; we just needed to be extra careful, that was all. Extra careful. And extra clear, too. Clear, clear. There was no room now for doing anything that might be interpreted in any other way, in any unintended way. I was completely at ease concerning this. I didn't feel the slightest bit worried.

The boss didn't address anyone in particular when, without introduction, he suddenly said, "Well?"

At the time, I had been contemplating the knife, and so he startled me. I was afraid he might have noticed.

"Well? How long are we going to go on like this, begging you for the truth?"

I immediately looked in his direction, without looking him directly in the eye, telling him without words that I was ready and at his beck and call.

"What?" he added.

I kept looking toward him without looking him directly in the eye. Rather, I raised my sight slightly toward some part of him and then I lowered it, in order to say, "Okay. Let's get to it."

"You know, I've met a lot of assholes in my life, but none as bad as you!" the same one added after looking me over up and down. There was no way my wife didn't hear that, because it was happening right there in the kitchen, but she just kept herself occupied with the coffee pot as though the words that had reached her ears were commonplace and uninteresting. Was my wife that good at playing the game?

I wanted to smile when he said that. I wanted to smile like a powerful man, like a powerful, wise, and extremely patient man who could not be affected in the least by the words of those creatures who inhabit and scuttle about the mere surface of this earth. But when I saw that she didn't pay any attention, I thought I would save us their smug reactions for some other time when my wife was prepared for it. So I didn't smile. I said to myself, "Let me concern myself with the most important thing—what more could I say that would satisfy them and still be the truth?"

This bewildered me. What could I possibly say? What more could I say? I had already told them everything I knew, and answered all their questions. I had emptied out my entire memory to them. Completely, so what else was there? Certainly there were things I remembered while telling them everything I remembered, but which I didn't tell them, and that was intentional, because I didn't want to tell them about... like... for example... the time I cheated on my wife. That was none of their business. I mean, it was of no use to them. So I hid it from them with a clear conscience. Nor did my concealing it pose any danger to me, because they didn't know anything about it, nor could they know... Unless they were gods who could read minds. But I don't think so.

"Don't you think we know everything, especially about you?"

Could they possibly know about something that happened that even the light of day didn't know about? Could they

111

possibly keep an eye on everyone, all day long, around the clock? It had been a holiday, and we were having lunch at my wife's parents' house. We realized we had forgotten to bring the baby's formula. He was only a few months old, and it was up to me to go home and get it. So I went. While I was looking for it in the kitchen, the doorbell rang, so I went to open the door, wondering who it could be, and also thinking about what a coincidence it was—I had only been there seconds—I opened the door to find a beggar woman saying, "God bless you, Mister… and give you good health… and bless your children…."

I told her I only had one child. Then I added, "I don't have any money," and started to shut the door in her face, because she wasn't going to leave on her own. But she blocked me from shutting the door with her hand. I was surprised. That was not something beggars did.

Then she said, "I'll do whatever you want, just give me money, God bless you, I am a desperate woman."

So I said, "Like what?"

She came closer, slowly, saying, "Whatever you want!" Now she was all the way in and had shut the door behind her while repeating, "Whatever you want." That woman bewitched me. I don't know what she sprinkled over me to strip me of my willpower. Seeing me standing there bewildered, she reached for my pants and carried on until I gave her the reaction she was trying for. Then I gave her what she wanted and she disappeared. So, were they the kind of people who sent these kinds of women to get people in trouble and hold them hostage to blackmail? (Do they teach these women to take pictures?) Could it be? If that was the case, then I had better tell them, so as not to be accused of concealing information, or of being selective about what information I was willing to give.

"What makes you think you can be selective, you...! Don't you know we have things you can't even imagine? Want us to show you pictures?"

Then the boss sighed and said like a know-it-all, "Why don't you tell your wife about your infidelity?" Then, after a short pause he added, "Mr. Good Husband."

At this point I won't hide for one second that I was shocked, but I understood exactly how important it was to stay in control of myself. I told myself I had to be stronger than they were. They were just trying to break me down by claiming that they had everything, but they didn't actually have everything. No power exists that has everything. Furthermore, their calculations were pretty simple. The chances that I had cheated on my wife, even if only once, were very high, considering the high percentage of men who do that. So I said, "I don't cheat on my wife." I said it clearly, calmly, sincerely, and without provocation.

"You'll have to pardon us, Imm... (He used my son's name here) but your husband has forced us to have to use inappropriate language." Then he explained saying, "Inappropriate for you to hear, and inappropriate to be used in your presence."

Then he went on, "But tell us, please, how a nice woman like you can stand living with such a person."

"Everyone has their lot in life," my wife said.

Oh my God! My wife's answers that day really shocked me. How could she say such things, which were so ambiguous, and open to so much interpretation. It could easily be understood that I was completely unworthy of her and that they were absolutely right in their estimation of me; they had figured out the real me in an instant. Indeed, that was exactly what they would understand from it; it was the most obvious interpretation.

What else does it mean when you say to a woman, "Your husband is no good," and she replies, "That's my lot in life!" She should have kept quiet, not said anything, especially since there was nothing forcing her to reply, nothing forcing her to say anything, or answer at all, and especially since they had yet to interpret anything she said according to anything but their own whims. They weren't about to understand what she said as meaning, for example, a way of using their own logic against them to undermine it. I'm not sure my wife really understood how important her role was at this point, and the effect every word she said had on the course of events, because basically she was innocent and had no idea what was going on. I mean, what was going on in the country in general, too, which was very dangerous, and which was reflected in every aspect of society. (Women should be required to follow politics like men.) So my wife, in simplest terms, was taking in what was happening to us on a purely personal and ethical basis, as some shameful act being committed against us, all because some people made us welcome them into our house against our will, at a time they chose, and in an inappropriate way. And my wife couldn't forget the fact that she was the daughter of respectable people, for generations on end, and no person existed who could possibly outbrag her, or point out any defect in her behavior. Indeed, the person who would dare to justifiably insult her was yet to be born. She believed the very axis around which the earth spins would be knocked off balance if anyone dared touch her honor—and the honor of her home was of course part and parcel of her personal honor, and her husband's honor, too. They were one and the same. ("I'll tell my father!" she'd say whenever she had any difficulties or anyone bothered her.) Life had yet to test my wife enough. That was why she was not very good at dealing with these critical situations with the wisdom and patience they required. The world, unfortunately, was not as she thought. The world can not be cut with a knife—as the proverb goes—and the winds blow as they please, not according to the wishes of the sailboat.

At this point, the bell rang—the doorbell, and I hoped it was her parents. This was the second time the doorbell rang. The first time the person ringing was not persistent. But this time he was. Had she tried to contact someone somehow and told him or her what was happening to us? Had she been able to tell one of our friends or relatives?

Her parents rarely came at this time, but sometimes they did, in order to see their beloved grandson before he went to bed. Had they called and got worried when no one answered and came over to put their minds at ease? I hoped so.

As for our guests, they didn't move. They acted as if they hadn't heard anything. Then, after a few more tries, the ringing stopped. It must not have been her parents then, or else they would have called out, and pounded on the door.

I looked at her over at the sink when the doorbell rang. She was very alert, her ears perked, but she didn't turn to look at all, nor did she give any indication that she cared, or hoped, or was affected. Strange. Did she have the game in her hands to such an extent, with such sharp cleverness? (This experience would strengthen our marriage, bring us closer together forever more. We would certainly pass this test, which would become mere memories, memories we would recall during hard times in order to overcome them.)

"Okay. Now what?" he said.

"Here's your coffee. Enjoy it."

She interfered at exactly the right time, rescuing me from the problem of speaking without words. Every time they had asked such a question I was unsure of what to say, so I would fidget and look around, sometimes landing my sight on his body— never his eyes—to let him know I was ready for any questions and ready to assist in any way. All he had to do was start. As for whether he was expecting me to divulge what he wanted on my own, what was I supposed to divulge? What?

I admit that at one point I made a mistake, and thereby gave him the notion that given the right moment or the right place I might talk. That was when I told him that sometimes when I'm busy with something else, or if I'm in a certain place, I suddenly remember some matter I have forgotten, or some thing, some event, or a name. So did he get the idea that maybe I was hiding some nice big surprise for him, which would come in due time, and therefore he decided to accompany me along with his buddies to my house? What was it, then, that I said and don't remember anymore that made him think that my house would be the right place and this evening the right time? Was it just one more instance of my taking a step in a direction I didn't want to go? God! When, oh when will my steps lead me where I'm headed? And when will my emotions develop according to my desires? Was it really something I said that led them to my house, to the very heart of my personal life and into its very innards, when all I really meant was a fact that gets repeated day in and day out, which is that you try to remember a name, but to no avail, so you try really hard, but still to no avail, then you forget about it and after a while, which may be long or may be short, the name just comes to you all of a sudden while you're occupied with other matters, God knows where. That's all I wanted to say to them and it is true. How could it be understood any other way? How could it hold any meaning other than the one I intended and specified to him? It seems talk is just like the ringing of a bell; everyone hears it however he or she wants and claims it is saying something different.

Could it have been I—my self—who led them to my house? Did they tell my wife that, or something like that? Did they give her that impression? Did they whisper something to her? What exactly did they drop into her ear?

Is that why every so often I got the feeling she was about to blow up at me? Is that why she wouldn't look me in the eye? Is that why she didn't serve me until the very last, after serving everyone else? She served everyone except me. Or had she done that because she knew I couldn't eat with my mouth all cut up and my front teeth broken. But she never came close enough to me to get a good look. (Did they tell her?) Didn't my wife know that a person in this condition—my condition—should be coaxed into eating to gain back his strength and be able to face the situation he was in? Especially the kind of situation I was in. Such a person is in terrible need of strength and determination and desire and will—yes, the will to live! In order to be able to conquer the situation and get out of it with the least damage possible.

"Here's sugar for anyone who wants it."

"I don't drink it unless it's sweetened in the pot!" This voice came from inside, from the bedroom, as if from someone scolding his wife, and it was like a stick of dynamite had exploded in my head.

No! No! Everything has a limit. Everyone has a limit, no matter how high his or her station or great his or her abilities.

No doubt he was lying on the bed in there, with his shoes off. (It was mild, spring weather, not cold, not hot.) Did he want my wife to bring him his coffee in there? No! No! That was stepping over the line. After my wife poured coffee for everyone at the table, me among them, the boss said, "One more!"

My wife said the coffee was black, no sugar (in other words, not the way the other one liked it.)

"We can't drink by ourselves," he said (meaning to remind my wife of the one on the bed.) "You know that; you're the perfect hostess!"

So my wife got up, put the pot back on the stove, and boiled what was left in it after adding a spoonful of sugar, in order to cater to the one inside.

"Drink!" said my neighbor to me.

I told him I like sugar in my coffee (lucky for me), and he said you couldn't drink it without sugar. It was difficult for me to spoon out the sugar with that tiny spoon and stir it without tipping the cup. In fact, it almost tipped over many times, and each time I hoped my wife would come to my rescue, but she didn't, despite the fact that she heard my neighbor threatening me and swearing to me that if I spilled the coffee on the table, or on him (especially on him!—"I'll bathe you with the whole pot!") I really wanted a cup of coffee at the time; I love coffee in the evening after dinner. Indeed, I can't fall asleep, unlike many, many people, without it. After I was finally able to sweeten my cup of coffee without too much damage, I lifted it to my lips, but I couldn't sip anything, because my lips were swollen. So I put it back in front of me on the table without saying anything. When my neighbor saw me do that, he became irritated, and his eyes opened wide and round. He didn't stay like that very long before suddenly making me get up. He ordered me to take my pants off, out of the blue, and he hit me over the head, but I decided I would not take my pants off. I decided to make this a line of defense I would not retreat from no matter what. I did not take them off. And I would not take them off. Everything has a limit beyond which life just isn't nice anymore. They could take from me whatever they wanted, and I was ready to cooperate with them to the furthest extent, but *that* was not going to be repeated *here*. I was prepared at that moment to explode, like a bomb packed tightly with highly explosive materials, like one of those incredible bombs that used to go off in the middle of the street during traffic hour in Beirut and mow down people and places. Yes, right that second. Earlier I was saying that this event would come to an end sooner or later, and it wasn't worth dying over, but now, forget it! Things had come to a head!

Just then my wife came over, picked up the boss's coffee cup, took a sip, and then another sip. Then she put it back down on the table. After a little while she went over to the second man and took a sip of his coffee, and from the third man's, too. Then she poured the other cup and took a sip from that one, too. She hadn't poured herself a cup to begin with; she never drinks coffee in the evening, but now she poured herself a cup and sat down next to the boss to drink it.

"What are you so upset about? What's gotten into you?" the boss said reproachfully to my neighbor, with a tinge of reprimand in his voice. Then he looked at my wife and said as if apologetically trying to clarify things, "Work, work, work. It's exhausting."

A new development. That was a new development.

That was a new development I hadn't seen at all before. Very positive. The first of its kind since the whole mess began. It might just be signaling a turn for the better. But, I said to myself, I had to stay calm and not go overboard with optimism. Calm. No mistakes now.

Then he picked up his coffee cup and brought it to his lips, but before taking a sip he said, as if suddenly remembering something, "What about our man inside?"

At the time I was sitting down again, after the positive interference from the boss. So, in response to his question, and having been encouraged by the positive development that had taken place, as well as that semi-apology of his, and as well by the fact that I had sat down of my own volition after being made to stand up by my neighbor, without any opposition from anyone and furthermore, and this is very important, this was the first time any of them had spoken to any of the others in such a manner, which held the possibility that the whole situation might have changed, or was about to change… So, responding to the boss's question, "What about our man in the bedroom?" I said, "I'll take it to him."

"You'd like to take a little stroll while we're here working our butts off? We really have to put an end to this. Enough already!" He said that with his voice raised, and with unexpected irritation, especially since there had been signs that things were starting to settle down. Then, respectfully, he put his hand on my wife's thigh and said to her, "You solve the problem."

Actually, my wife had already started to get up when he asked her to solve the problem, having immediately understood that the task was hers. (Strange! Something about my wife had really started to bewilder me, ever since she replied so irritably that last time. She wasn't making any mistakes at all anymore, always acting at the right time, in the right way.) And so she carried the cup of coffee to him—the man in the bedroom—and didn't come back.

She stayed there with him.

Or maybe she headed to the living room, and stayed there a

while by herself to catch her breath a little, and dream up some miracle that would get us out of that mess, which seemed set on dragging us to our total demise.

That possibility—that she was by herself—was more likely than its alternative—that she was with him—because no sound, noise, or anything from there reached us out in the kitchen.

"So!" the boss said before pausing patiently.

"This is the last time I will ask you to speak. Do you hear me? So speak now, or you'll see and hear things that will not please you at all! Is that clear?"

Strange. He said, "You'll see and hear...!" as if he wanted to hurt me through someone else other than me directly. What did he mean? Through whom? (Through whom!)

I didn't answer his question, but he persisted, repeating for a second time with increased resolve. "Is that clear?"

"Yes. Clear," I said.

"Then let's go. You will not waste one more second, or else you'll pay dearly for it. We've been respectful to you in front of your wife. You saw for yourself how nicely we treated your wife in front of you and how respectful we were to her. We were being as cooperative and considerate with you as possible, so return the favor, or half as much at least. Unless you're a total good-for-nothing with absolutely no sense of decency."

I said, "So be it."

It was time we finished this whole ordeal, I said to them. Right now, once and for all. And I asked them, as a way of showing them both my good intentions and my insistence on putting an end to this tragi-comedy, to define clearly exactly what it was they wanted to know from me, so I wouldn't get carried away in my telling of things and go on and on in vain, and end up rousing their ire like every other time, and then have to start all over again. That method was not working anymore. We had to replace it with a more effective one, because the time had come and we were all sick and tired of chewing on hay.

"Here we go again!" the boss said, disgusted and obviously very angry.

At this point I heard my wife suddenly scream and then fall silent. I wondered if it came from the bedroom or the living room. Were they hurting the boy? Then I heard her say, "My son! My darling son!"

I was right, and had been afraid for good reason... the boy! Oh God! Oh God! Oh God! What had given them the impression that the house would be more conducive to getting information out of me than the office or the interrogation room? But before I started to get up I noticed, fortunately, that my wife had clearly become suspiciously silent. As if her voice was recorded on a tape and came and went at the touch of a button... Did my wife still have everything under control like an expert who knows how to bend just far enough to avoid being broken, or who knows which string to pull, which to loosen, in order to keep everything from slipping from her hands?

Or was my wife...

Or was my wife still convinced (they convinced her) that I was guilty and should confess. In which case, she too was of the mind that every available means be used—all means—to force me to confess.

Did they really convince her that I was an unfit husband? Those riffraff were capable of convincing her of anything they wanted. No!

I said, "I swear to you by everything dear to me, on my honor and..."

I wanted to continue by saying, "and my wife's honor and my son's life!" But he didn't let me finish. He interrupted me and jeered, "On your honor? You're swearing on your honor when you've been getting fucked all day long?"

I deserved that. Yes, I deserved those words. Wasn't I the one who exposed myself to that stab? So, let me admit to being no good at anything. What on earth made me use the word honor? If I'd only thought about it a second before making that ridiculous oath, I'd have predicted their response. Idiot. Idiot! He was expecting it. So let me admit to being a total jackass nothing. The only thing I'm good at is making things worse.

Then I heard my wife's voice a second time, screaming for help, "My son! My baby! My pride and joy!"

So my wife was good at acting. She was good at acting, radio drama especially. She, too, wanted to pressure me into confessing. That was clear as day. But confess what? What was I supposed to confess? What, God? What?

Fine.

I said to them and made certain to them that this time was going to be different from before, and it would be the last time, too.

"Here we go again," the boss repeated. "Right back where we started."

At this point my neighbor approached me, stood with his torso right in my face, and pulled my head toward him. My neighbor was a pig. Then he reached his hand to it. I'll kill him, I said to myself. I'll kill them all, but he's first, the son of a bitch.

Then, suddenly, the miracle happened.

"You must be exhausted now, so go rest a bit in bed. Sleep for an hour or two. We'll go and come back after that. But only on one condition, that you promise us once and for all that you are going to tell the truth and nothing less than the truth."

Then he repeated what he said when he saw me so surprised, my mouth gaping like an idiot.

But I heard him fine the first time.

This, then, was another new development, I thought. No, more than a new development. This was a miracle! Could it be? What were they scheming? What was their strategy, and what trap were they hoping I would step into? Then I saw they were getting ready to leave. Yes, they were really going! I saw that as best I could with my eyes. They were ready to leave, but they were missing one thing—the fourth man whom I had not seen yet and whom I was really hoping to see. He'd become a phantom. They guessed what was going through my mind and said to me, "Thursday."

What was that supposed to mean? "Thursday!" Then they hadn't guessed what was going through my mind after all. Why this talk about days? Why Thursday of all days? Strange. (Or maybe I wasn't thinking straight anymore.)

"Of course, of course, he's going with us."

Oh my God! Were they mind readers? Were they connected directly to my brain? "Tell the truth, then, man," I said to myself. "Tell the truth without delay."

I said, "You want the truth and nothing but the truth. Well, here it is:

"I did not have any connection to that man (I meant the man in the picture) close or distant. I didn't like him and didn't hate him either. I had never even heard of him. I knew only that he existed. I knew he was there and nothing more. I didn't follow his activities or even know he had any activities. I didn't know his positions on things. Actually, I was surprised to find out what they were later on..." The boss interrupted me here,

124

and asked me what I meant by this last statement. What exactly did I mean by "surprised?" (There was no avoiding a mistake. Man is a mistake-maker, that's all there is to it.) And what were these positions I was so surprised by? And was I pleasantly surprised or unpleasantly surprised? I told him everything would become clear soon enough. I was able to direct my words the way I wanted, which gave me the strength and confidence I so desperately needed.

"I was surprised by these positions, as I was saying, and by what they entailed, because I never knew how much influence he had. I still have no way of knowing that exactly even now because the elements necessary to allow you to know as much as you want and as much as would allow you to feel at ease, are unavailable at this time, for reasons everyone knows."

"What do you do besides your regular occupation?" the boss interrupted, confusion all over his face. I answered that that was unimportant, especially since everything would become clear in good time.

"Let's continue getting to the truth." I said to him.

So he quieted down. I was in charge now, as long as truth was in my hands. So I continued what I was saying. But at this point, unfortunately, I started to feel in more pain than before, contrary to what I expected, which was that it would subside a little bit at least, since I had gotten some relief emotionally from the enormous pressure that was weighing down on me. I thought that the power that came with revealing the truth would ease my pain. But unfortunately, matters proceeded against my expectations and hopes.

"Anyway," I continued, "It was difficult for me to know, therefore, the way I usually hope to know when it has to do with something that concerns me, I mean like... I'm sure you know what I mean," I said to him, so he wouldn't think the person in the picture was like some person I didn't care about, or was insignificant, or that what he believed in, for example, was...So he cut in saying, "Sure, sure!" In other words, my meaning was quite clear to him.

"I was surprised."

I was surprised at that moment, too, because it, too, was a new, positive development, totally unexpected. It was as though he were listening like a friend, making things easy and not taking words at face value, but rather according to their intended meaning. And a friend's intended meaning is usually something good, otherwise he wouldn't be a friend. Strange. So what was going on? Did they receive some kind of communication about us? Had they been told to be nice to us, finish up the matter quietly and politely, and then leave? Strange.

Then I continued with the truth, "I admit, then, that I didn't like him, and I definitely didn't hate him. But I didn't like him."

"Okay. But why didn't you like him? What about him didn't you like?"

"But I didn't hate him."

"Okay. Okay. But we're asking why you didn't like him."

Actually, I don't know why I didn't like him. I never really thought about it. It never crossed my mind. Anyway, I rarely even heard about him. Maybe I never heard of him at all before. One thing was sure. When what happened to him happened and I heard about it, I wasn't surprised—I mean, I wasn't surprised at all to hear that the person whom that happened to existed. Sometimes you do get surprised someone exists, you know, like when someone tells you so-and-so's daughter got married and you're surprised and say, does so-and-so have a daughter?

I told them all of that very frankly, and I think they appreciated my frankness.

"But we're still exactly where we started concerning the question, which is, why didn't you like him? Especially since you weren't surprised to know he existed when…"

I cut in here, intentionally, because I didn't want them to say outright what happened to him. I mean, what happened to him has a name, and I didn't want them to mention the name of that thing that happened—say it and it'll come true! I was superstitious about that, and saw it as an omen of black moments to come, so I interrupted them and said, "Yes. I wasn't surprised he existed in the world. That's correct."

"So, he existed in your mind, in your consciousness, and you didn't like him, so why? Answer the question. We're getting dizzy from all this talking in circles."

I wanted to answer here by saying that a person's feelings toward lots of people can sometimes be neutral, or unconcerned, but I was mindful of the fact that a person like him, or—let's call things what they are—a "personality" like him, well, it's hard for a person to feel neutral or unconcerned toward him, as they might feel toward any random person walking around the earth on two legs. So how would they believe me, then? One minute I was forgetting the name of a person I had just greeted with warmth and enthusiasm, another minute I was forgetting the name of a person whose number I wrote in my address book, another minute I was forgetting a person completely, even though his name was clearly written in my address book, and the next minute I was having neutral, unconcerned feelings toward some other person who was not at all like other people, who was extraordinary...what next?

As for the watch, they didn't ask me anything about it. When I wanted to tell them the story, they refused to listen, totally, just as they refused to listen when I wanted to tell them my name. Strange. (And they didn't ask my wife's name either. They were content with just calling her "Imm so and so" and nothing more.)

I admit I'm not the highly believable type. I also admit at the same time that I was telling the truth. And that was precisely my predicament. If only the matter rested on me and me alone, and was limited to me and me alone, but I dragged my wife and my son into it. I was not alone, therefore, and that was why I was convinced even more than before of the necessity to cooperate with them as much as possible, and the need to open my heart, mind, home, and everything in my possession to them in order to change their opinion of me and win their trust. Then, and only then, would they be able to believe me.

But unfortunately they were being extremely cautious with me, and what they were now about to find out about me (and from me) didn't encourage them to let down their guard. The infernal circle! How to break out of it? How?

My wife! My wife had to be the way in to regaining their trust, and consequently the solution. The solution was in her hands; she alone was capable of it. But how...how could my wife regain their trust, reestablish their respect for me, and retain my dignity simultaneously?

"You haven't asked about your wife since she left! You are a strange creature. Selfish. You don't care about anything but your own self. Didn't you hear her scream?"

"She's acting."

"She's acting!" I said. Then I paused for a second to make

sure I really heard myself saying that, that I actually said it myself—my very self—then I continued of my own accord, when there was no reason to continue. As if the words dragged themselves out and went wherever they willed. I said, "I didn't know she was so good at acting. Especially radio drama."

They looked at me with complete confusion and bewilderment, as if to say, "Has this guy gone crazy? Or does he really want to pawn off his wife for us to leave him alone." This was exactly what their demeanor was saying, because they did not hesitate much at all before asking me unabashedly, so I answered that everything had its limit. I answered them calmly, but with strength and determination. They answered with a nod that showed they understood, and that they agreed with what they understood. But at the same time, I sensed a bit of mockery in the nod. So I wanted to be clearer, because they did not hesitate to understand anything originating from me or from my wife however they wanted or found useful to them.

"I'm serious," I added.

They said they were certain of that.

But this time, too, there was some mockery in what they said. Or, maybe more likely there was a kind of message in it that meant, "Yes. We understand." (Meaning they understood what they wanted.) But what? What did they understand beyond what I said, which was that everything had its limit, and that for a person to cross these limits, at which he should stop, is undesirable and could lead to problems, or worse. That's what I meant by what I said. What else could they have understood?

As for whether they were insisting on believing I was trying to bargain with them, well that was very dangerous. (To me, of course, because it would entail making a clear proclamation of guilt.) Therefore, in order to jump these hurdles I found it necessary to repeat to them that I meant what I said; there was no room for interpretation.

"Serious!"

"What are you repeating for? We got the picture. You're serious. In fact, it's important to us that you be serious, because that way we can make progress in our work. But, we don't think she would agree with what you said."

"Agree?"

Agree with what? And why? I had said negative things about her, so why ask her to agree?

I had made a big mistake, no doubt about it, by saying what I said. But it wasn't the first mistake, nor was it to be the last... Yes it was!

It just might have been the last mistake...might have been the last mistake.

"No, we don't think she is as you said. The one thing we're sure of, though, is that you are a born liar. That's just something in you. Part of you."

Dearly I would pay for what my self had committed against me. Both!

I got tangled up in *both* vices at the same time: trying to bargain and being guilty. I wanted to make a deal because I was guilty. Damn! Damn me and the day I was born, and a day to come (soon) in which I would die (now?). Damn those who bore me into this world, and damn those who bore them! Damn you, Father! Damn you, Mother! What kind of upbringing did you give me?

"I mean that there are limi..." I wanted to say "limits," but they interrupted me.

"You take two steps forward and three steps back, two steps forward, three steps back, that's how it's been from the

130

beginning of the journey, which is why we don't get anywhere and never will. From the moment you promised and swore you would tell the truth and then started going off on a tangent… and now you offer us something, and when you got scared and found us (us!) defending your wife, you retreated, and went on repeating over and over, "Serious. Serious." To no end. So tell us what you want, then, and where you're leading us. Be clear. Have you forgotten we're not here to play around, or to waste time, but to find out right now who tore the picture? So who tore the picture, you fucking asshole? Son of a bitch!"

All right. Let them insult me all they wanted, but not my mother! They had no right to insult her. That really hurt, to be called a son of a bitch. I had cursed them out of anger, but *they* had done it out of spite.

"Bend over, bastard!"

I actually never stopped telling the truth. They pushed me with their questions into talking about other things. I told them that, but they didn't like it. They said they resorted to asking questions when they saw I wasn't telling them anything. So I said, then let me continue. There wasn't anything preventing me. On the contrary, I was still quite ready. So take back the son of a bitch thing. (I don't think my wife saw anything, but I'm not completely sure.)

"Listen! Speak and save your wife instead of ranting and raving about her."

So I said very quickly, in order not to waste any time, and in order to save my wife from this hell (the hell after death was a photocopy, I was sure, of what was happening there now on earth) I said, "I didn't like him!"

And they laughed. They burst into laughter, because they thought I hadn't divulged anything.

"We're right back where we started! Where did we get with that? What's new? We've known you don't like us for a long time. Tell us who tore the picture, and don't tell us about your feelings toward us because we know and we don't want to hear about it."

They didn't want to know my feelings about the picture, and that was all there was to tell. That was the one and only truth I wanted to lead them to; I had no other. It was the end of the end. That was all I had. Blessed are those who can keep up the fight beyond this stage. As for me, this is where I surrendered. All I had to reveal was that that picture irritated me every time I passed by it, and I was always afraid my self might surprise me by going up to it and tearing it in anger. I used to avoid looking at it in order not to be attracted to it like a moth that is unavoidably attracted to the light and dies. I used to be afraid of that picture, very afraid, to the extent that I sensed it was evil.

"You're still talking to us about your feelings, and that's the last thing we care about."

Then I told them outright that I don't like pictures of the deceased to be hung like that on walls, no matter who they are, and no matter how they died. I don't like for people to have to look at them day after day, forcibly. Yes! That's the way I feel, plain and simple. What does it mean for me to be forced to see the picture of a martyr, for example, or of a bridegroom who spent his wedding night in some tragic accident, or of a child killed by blind hatred, or drowned in a flood, or buried in an earthquake! What does it mean, and why? Does it mean the lost loved one is so very dear and that you are like his parents and should receive condolences, affection, appreciation, and tribute, and everything connected with a great loss?

"Spare us your hot air now and just tell us who tore the picture."

There was no way I could tell him I didn't know. That answer had already cost me a lot, so I had to think up something new. (I always had to think up something else to say whenever I was asked this question.) I thought about how to answer them, but finding a different answer all the time for the same question is not a simple matter. And I was completely immersed in my worries when I heard them saying—saying to me, "You're exhausted now. Go rest a while in bed; sleep an hour or two. We'll go and come back later, but only under one condition, that you promise us once and for all that you are going to tell the truth and nothing less than the truth."

Another new development, I said. Could it be? What kind of trick were they up to? What was their strategy? What was this trap they wanted me to step into? Then I saw them getting ready to leave. Yes, they were really going! I saw that best I could with my eyes. They were ready to leave, but they were missing one thing—the fourth man whom I hadn't seen yet, and whom I was really hoping to see. He'd become a phantom. They guessed what was going through my mind and said to me, "Don't worry. Just promise us, and don't forget that 'a free man's promise is binding.'"

I hesitated in answering the question, because I wondered how I could fulfill the promise if I made it? Especially since I already divulged what I had been hiding from them. They heard what I had to say and didn't want to listen. Not because it irritated them, but because they considered it insignificant and not worth listening to. And that was the extent of my surprise for them, and it had taken all they did to me to make me say it and admit to it. And here they were now making fun of it.

Strange. What was going on now that I didn't understand? What had impaired my ability to comprehend? I, who always take great pride in my intelligence. Then the truth suddenly flashed in my mind: they were intruders.

They were trespassing against me and the inhabitants of my home, and against my home, too. That was precisely the truth of what was happening.

It was trespassing!

They were intruders, and I had to deal with them on that basis. Any method I used to fight them off I would be able to defend as my inalienable right before any official body, or any individual, or any institution. Not only that, they never even identified themselves to me, never showed me any papers or badges explaining who they were and what they were doing. Therefore, with a simple calculation, I figured out that I should make them leave the house so I could catch my breath and get everything ready before they came back. First of all, I had to figure out a way for my wife and son to escape. (Oh God! Was that possible?)

Never before had I thought of keeping a gun. But everything has its moment. If only I had a gun then, I would have been the happiest man in the world.

"Watch it!"

Really? They knew I was thinking about a gun?

I was so startled, so startled. How did they guess? They had just finished guessing my desire to see the fourth one leave with them. Could they read minds? Did they use their magical methods to figure out what I was planning to do while they were away?

"It's not out of concern for you that we're telling you to watch it, you know. It's to free us of any blame. See, you can't get us, but we can get you, in case you think it would be easy to…"

Yes, it was possible.

Hadn't they been reading my thoughts from the start of the day and stripping me naked, piece by piece, and opening up the very spot in my body and in my memory that they wanted?

Hadn't they known about what happened between the beggar woman and me and exposed me in front of my wife? (I had no choice at all but to confess the truth! Because I'm one of those people who simply is unable to defy the truth. It's the one thing in this world I completely surrender to.) I saw how her eyes grew wide and welled up with tears. But I would be able to convince her later on that I just said that to them at the time, "So you could play a positive, active role!"

When they were just about to leave, my wife was among them, ready to go, too. I was not mistaken at all about that, for I saw her in outdoor clothes, with her purse, and everything she puts on or takes along when she leaves her house. There was absolutely no way I could not figure out what my wife was doing: she was leaving my house.

(If only I had a gun!)

Speaking of that, how did they know I *didn't* have a gun in the house without making a search? How had they been so sure and confident about that? They knew there were no weapons, then, or else they would have searched. Who told them what was there and what wasn't there? Could it have been some other person not related to us, a stranger?

So my wife wanted to accompany them. Why? Was she afraid of me? Afraid I would blame her for things, or attribute things to her, or what?

Did she, too, see evil in my eyes? Did she guess what I was intending to do? Or had they convinced her, and what exactly had they convinced her of? That I was a monster? That I was a creature unworthy of her? And what about our son? There she was all ready to go out with them on her own, without the boy. Oh god of tribulations, help me. Did she want to abandon me and every last trace of me, including my son, the fruit of her womb? Had they convinced her that I was behind all the widespread decadence in the universe? Had they shown her pictures? (I don't remember seeing them take pictures.)

If only I could get my hands on some kind of weapon right now, I could quench my thirst for revenge. I have heard of people, entire nations in fact, trying to emulate their executioners, and women falling in love with them, but there was no way this could happen to my wife. I was sure of her. I knew her inside and out. No way. But she was on her way out with them, alone, without her son, without anything else. She had nothing but the clothes she was wearing. I wanted to ask her with scorn and suffering (and with meanness, too) whether she was planning to burn her clothes after she left, too, to rid herself of all traces of evil. I would have said dirt or shame, but the words just wouldn't come. I didn't feel compelled to say it, so I just kept quiet and didn't ask her anything at all. What is the point of asking when you already know everything and more?

But what would she say to her parents? How and what would she tell them about what happened? And what would they say to her? Would they say, "You did the right thing! Our first impression of him was right, and we didn't hide it, either, when he asked for your hand in marriage. We told you he was not worthy of you. You didn't want to believe us. At any rate, leaving him now is better than later, because it was going to happen sooner or later. And if he wants, let him keep his seed!" And then they would flood her with kisses and affection and sympathy and she would sob with delight and gratitude.

And they would just forget all about the boy. I would have to look after him all by myself, because my parents are so far away. Fine! I accept the challenge.

But before they left, with her, they told me not to go into the living room at all, because they left some things in there that were their business and no one else's, especially not mine. They didn't want anyone looking at them or going near them. They said if I went in there they would consider it a breach in the agreement we had. In fact, they would consider it sabotage of their mission and a clear act of aggression against them and what they represented. They insisted on hearing a clear statement from me expressing that I would not go in there, so I wouldn't try to claim later on that I hadn't made any such promise, and also to clarify what my obligations were in case I broke the promise, especially since I was so adept at shirking responsibility. They said that last part (the boss said it if I remember correctly) with the confidence of experienced experts. They had gotten to know me well, having spent a whole day having to deal with me.

I believe I enunciated my promise loudly and clearly.

Then they left. They asked me to turn around so they could make their exit in safety. So I turned around and faced the sink while they left. My sight fell upon two items: the big knife and the barbecue skewers.

It would be an act of self-defense, I said. An inalienable right under all legal systems, jurisprudence, and religions. No one would blame me for it, nor would I be required to apologize to anyone. On the contrary.

But, my wife's position would weaken mine. In fact, it would reduce me to a mere murderer. And my son could not testify (as a witness).

But I would find a way. I could not surrender. That was not my nature. My nature was about endurance, patience, and struggle.

What about the telephone? Was I allowed to answer it and make calls while they were gone? I didn't ask them. The first thing that happened after they left was the phone. It rang! So what should I do? Should I answer? Maybe they were calling. I was convinced of that when the doorbell rang. Were they trying to test me? Was my wife on the line and they wanted to hear what I would say to her? For that matter, the worst predicament on earth is to have your wife against you, especially when you're in dire need of her like I was. I didn't answer the phone. I let it ring. It rang a lot until it finally got tired and stopped.

My son first. I said the first thing I had to do was check on my son, but I couldn't get up from the chair. It was as though something was preventing me from moving. The pain was only average. I mean, it wasn't screaming pain like having an electric wire poked into your testicles. (Speaking of that, if I had to choose between being poked by such a wire in the testicles, the penis, or inside the ear, I definitely would not choose inside the ear.) So the pain allowed for movement, but I could not get up. Then, and maybe because it had taken so much effort, I felt as if someone or more than one person was helping me to get up and walk to the bedroom to see my son in his little bed, lying down with his eyes closed (asleep?).

I wanted to go closer to him, but they didn't let me, claiming I might wake him up and he wouldn't be able to get back to sleep, and they still had a lot of work ahead of them... So what was going on, then? Was I dreaming? Wasn't I alone? Didn't I see them leave, with my own two eyes? So how could I have the feeling they were still there, not letting me go near my son?

138

What was going on?

Oh, Mother, your son has gone insane! He has started seeing them there beside him and he talks to them. They even stop him from doing what he wants, even though he is all alone.

As for my wife, I didn't know where she was anymore, as if they had hidden her from me; as if they had dressed her in a magic cloak and now she was invisible to me. But I knew she was there, moving about nervously, trying to get away from me. Why was she so frightened of me, when I have never done anything from the moment I met her until now, until this very second, that was not in her interest.

When I went near my son's bed in the bedroom, I wished I could bend down and kiss him, so I could hear his breathing especially, because I was still worried about it after the tranquilizer he was forced to take to go to sleep right away, so they could create an atmosphere conducive to work. But when I started to bend down, I felt a sharp pain unlike the other pain I had felt earlier. It was a deep, profound pain that forced me to stand up straight. Then, when I went over to the bed—my wife's and mine—and raised my leg so I could lie down on the bed, I felt the intense pain again.

I wanted to pass by the living room to see who was in it before getting to the bedroom. Actually, to find out for sure whether or not my wife was in there. But that place was totally off-limits, for reasons mentioned to me but which I didn't understand at all, nor did I want to. Yes I did!

All that is veiled is coveted. This is an unshakable human trait. Even with a child, if you forbid something from him or her, he or she wants it all the more. But in dangerous situations a person must overcome his spontaneity and curiosity and leave matters up to the brain. I wanted to go into that room, not to see what was inside, but just like that, just to go inside. My desire to do it grew bigger and stronger to the point that I couldn't deny it. What encouraged it, too, was the freedom I felt having been left all alone. And what was more, it was a challenge, and I love a challenge. I love embarking into the unknown. It's a characteristic I took on as a child, and learned at school, but I didn't often get the chance to use. Now the opportunity was grand, so what was I waiting for? Go! But, before going into the room, I had to prepare the weapons I would use: the big knife and one of the skewers. I should hold the skewer in my hand, and tuck the knife in at my waist. That way I could strike with the skewer first, since it would be good for quick and easy stabbing. Okay. I would prepare the weapons first, and then go to the room, open the door, and go in, thus ready for any surprise. After all, I was not at all sure of their intentions.

So why lie down on the bed?

To rest. To rest!

Then, after I was able to raise one leg, I tried to raise the other, but couldn't—sure is a lucky thing a person has only two legs and not more, so he doesn't have to lift a larger number of them every time he wants to rest in his bed. Imagine a man with several legs tied to something and twisted up by force, as if they were pliable rods, and him screaming in pain. Or imagine a man with several testicles all tied together with a live wire. I think two legs are enough. And, one testicle. I mean, the strict minimum required to be a man, because two of everything doesn't necessarily double his pleasure, just as having only one penis doesn't lessen it.

I imagined myself sharing this philosophical observation with my friends. We would have laughed about it.

Then, as if something picked up my other leg and placed it on the bed, I had gotten completely onto the bed. But I was still sitting up and not yet lying down. It was as though some divine assistance kept watch over me, always. I don't know what I would have done without it. I lay back with great difficulty and pain, but not to sleep. Just to rest a little and think about how to carry out the plan with precision and efficiency, and without any mistakes. Let me begin, then, with defining exactly what the plan was: kill them one at a time when they came back. I would wait near the door, ready to open it for them. (Did they have a key? My wife threw her key at me onto the table just before I turned around so they could leave safely.) When the first one came in, I would stab him with the skewer, in through his stomach and out his back. Then I would swipe his gun from his waist as he fell to the floor, and shoot the rest of them before they knew what was happening. Surprise! The most important thing in these situations is the element of surprise; it was the determining factor and if I didn't take full advantage of it, I would fail and end up dying myself and getting my whole family killed along with me. Failure was strictly forbidden. Then, afterwards, I would turn myself in at the nearest police station. But just to be safe, I should call one of the newspapers, or contact some other media station, and tell them what I did before turning myself in, just in case! That way I would be covered no matter what.

From the beginning: the first one I would stab with the skewer. That matter was sure and simple. The second and the third—with the revolver (and the fourth). But there was a possibility something might go wrong during this part of the plan: was I sure I would be able to seize the revolver from the first one easily, before the other two stepped in and overtook me?

That was a very good question. And there was another thing, even more dangerous, and which would ruin the whole plan if it happened, that was if my wife came in first. There was a good possibility of that, too, because the people I was dealing with were no bunch of inexperienced kids. The possibility just might have occurred to them while they were doing their calculations. It must have. So now the question became whether they would dismiss it or not. And it was not totally out of the question that they would dismiss it, because they didn't give me much credit, in which case the element of surprise I would have as a result would have maximum effectiveness. But there was still the first possibility, which was that the two others might be able to grab me before I had a chance to get them, that is, before I managed to seize the revolver from the first one. There was a good possibility of that, as I already said. But such an operation could not be carried out without risks. All I could do was minimize them, guard against them. The best way to do that was to slam the door in their faces as soon as I stabbed him. That way I would have plenty of time to proceed to the succeeding stages. Take the revolver from his waist and shoot them through the door. I would have to memorize their positions and keep them in my mind while I was closing the door, in order not to miss. Then, as an added caution, I would open the door as quickly as possible (the surprise. The surprise! The most effective weapon!) as I was shooting them and check them to see if they had been hit yet. Then I would take aim and finish them off in a flash. Then I would take my wife, who would have backed out of the way upon hearing the first shot, into my arms, kiss her, and take her immediately into the house, to the bedroom, where the boy was, kiss him (would the gunshots wake him up?), pick him up and place him in his mother's arms and take them both out of

142

the house (none of the neighbors would come out before a few minutes had gone by—until they knew there was no more danger). Then I would get them into a taxi and send them to her parents while I headed for the police station. I couldn't forget to inform the media. That was very important. Because maybe the police were...Who knows! (Foreign media, of course.)

I thought the knife at my waist was going to be a hindrance, so what for? Why did I want to put it at my waist? Strange. It was as if without knowing it I were imitating someone or some custom I inherited and neglected to take a second look at, or as if I were yielding to some kind of revelation coming to me from some unknown place. I wasn't going to plunge into a battle in the usual way, with a dagger at my waist like in the old days. What was going to happen would be very unique. A short battle, out of self-defense, in the appropriate way, to stop an intruder. That kind of thing, nothing more.

After I stretched out a little, I realized I was very tired. I was worried I might fall asleep, so I decided I should get up. The mission ahead of me was going to be difficult, delicate, and dangerous. As I was in the process of getting up, my wife appeared to me, as if in a dream, though I wasn't dreaming. I was sure of that, more than sure. My wife appeared to me, and she had taken off her blouse to get ready for bed. Then she took off her skirt, standing as she usually did at these moments in front of the mirror. I opened my eyes good and wide—as best I could—to be certain of what I was seeing, but I didn't see anything. It was an apparition; a daydream. That was exactly what it must have been, couldn't have been anything else, because she wasn't there. I had seen her leave with them—she was the first one out—and I saw them follow out behind her.

It was an apparition. It was a daydream. It was whatever I wished it to be. (But I saw her trying to take something from the same dresser next to the bed, and that was not a dream.)

Time for action! No time for hallucinations. I must wait by the door, ready, or else my whole plan would fail. I would go get a chair, sit down, and listen, and if I heard their footsteps, I would get up. (Don't dare make any noise getting up from the chair.) But the living room was making me so curious. Why had it been forbidden? What had they put in there? Was one of them in there? (The fourth?) Eavesdropping on me and keeping surveillance? Was it locked, or was the door just shut, requiring a mere turn of the handle to be opened? I decided to get up and go to the door first. I would put my ear to it in case I could hear something, then at some later point, I would open the door calmly (or quickly?) turn on the light and see what it was that was in there that had been forbidden. (What was in there that I wasn't allowed to have?) Or had it been forbidden in order to decrease the amount of space I was allowed to move around in, thereby making me feel confined—so, yet another in the series of attempts meant to put pressure on me? Had there been some decision made about turning my house into a prison, and were the bedroom and the kitchen going to be off limits, too?

I would check on the living room, then, on my way to the door. Come what may. Knowing what was in that room was a necessary condition for the success of my plan; it may be from there that the fatal blow would come.

Why did I feel my hand on my belly when it was really on the bed? What a strange feeling. Whenever I was able to open my eyes, I was surprised to see it stretched out on the bed, when I was certain it was on my belly. I was sure I felt it there, weighing down on me. Strange. Yet when I opened and saw it was not on my belly, it was as if I were seeing some other hand of mine. And I felt my wife lying down beside me, her body touching against mine, and every time I opened my eyes to look at her I spontaneously closed them.

My wife's body seemed cold.

As if her body and the bed she was lying on were one, not two separate things.

As if the skewer in my hand secured her to the bed, never to be separated again.

Just a few of those pills that permitted them to do their work in peace were enough to put a child to sleep for God knows how long, forever. My son had been asleep for two days, but there was no need to worry if he was cold, because he was covered well. They could come whenever they wanted. I set up an atmosphere conducive to work, forever. But they should be aware it was conducive for me, too.

My wife's body got cold fast, even though it was spring and not winter.

I think I told them loud enough that there is a limit to everything. But they didn't understand, or they dismissed me as usual, and didn't give any value to what I said.

I had a pressing need to pee, so bad my teeth itched, but if I were to be granted what I wanted, I wouldn't be able to, whereas the first time...the first time there...anyway it seemed to me that I didn't quite remember anymore where the door to the bathroom was.

Mama!

It was as if the place was dissolving and blending together. The defining contours of thingss were getting all mixed up, or being erased, and it was difficult for me to remember the way to the bathroom door, or to imagine it, though my need was urgent and the urgency was increasing, but what was the point, whereas the first time...the first time...

The first time I was not allowed to swallow. I had to just swish it around in my mouth and spit it out, then starting all over, I had to

Afterword

Rashid al-Daif has said that he does not consider himself a novelist. Indeed, he resists calling himself a writer altogether. We assume that he means by this simply that he does not write from within the fictional tradition, that his explorations pursue other interests that we might call philosophical, psychological, epistemological, idiosyncratic.

We see his point. The books we have from him evade our grasp and leave us disoriented. Did the speaker of *This Side of Innocence*, that eccentric voice once referred to as "al-Rashid" (both "wise guy" and the author's name), tear the picture or didn't he? And whose picture was it and why was it illegal to tear it anyway? Al-Daif plays with the forms readers are used to (the novel of the unjustly accused citizen in a repressive government as in Orwell's *1984*, Sonallah Ibrahim's *The Committee* in Egypt, or F. M. Esfandiary's *Identity Card* in Iran), but with a focus that never allows us to visualize the society and offers us no more than tantalizing fragments of the story.

And yet there is a plot: the narrator has been arrested. We see him after an interrogation, in a very ordinary room. We watch him think so hard about the perfect, unassailable persona he is going to show the authorities that he almost gags trying to eat his address book, falls over and breaks a table when the phone rings.

That there is a mismatch between his interior world and the social world around him we become certain, and an atmosphere of violence that haunts the solitude could be the violence of authority. Or it could be his own. The fragmentary subplots are interesting in themselves, but they also divert the reader from the progression of events we want most to know about. The tutelary figure is Kafka, whom al-Daif mentions with enthusiasm in an interview by Aql al-Aweet in the newspaper *Al Nahar* on June 28, 1997. He compares his style to Kafka's, but contends it is "more brutal." He opposes Marquez, but only inasmuch as he considers him to have been a negative influence on the Arabic novel: "I felt (and I still do sometimes) that some Arabic novels have been written specifically for Marquez to read, or for his readers, at the very least."

But if the novelistic pleasures of *This Side of Innocence* are fragmented, the appeals that usher us into his fictional world are often precisely the pleasures we are used to in a more traditional novel. He is a master of suspense. A tiny paragraph can simply guarantee that we are going to keep turning the pages: "The light changed dramatically while I was wrapped up in all the writings and numerals. As if all of a sudden." At times the setting is recognizable and familiar, in the manner of a standard novel. When he is taken to a well-furnished room to be interrogated—"It was more like—compared with rooms and offices I had seen before—a lawyer's office. (I smiled when this idea came to mind.)"—we have the verisimilitude of an experience matched against a memory, but why a lawyer's office? And his smile, presumably at the incongruity of a lawyer's office as the setting for an interrogation, which he expects to be brutal, is psychologically acute and novelistic.

And the suspense implied in the setting (will it be a violent interrogation or won't it?) begs for resolution.

But the resolution doesn't arrive in the usual way. It just seems to arch further and further out into anticipation, in a dazzling tower of expectations. The story intensifies, even as it skips narrative cogs. We never see him tortured or even mistreated, but the reader senses an unspoken violation. In the harrowing concluding scenes, where the interrogators come to dinner, the horror almost materializes. Almost.

So if it is a novelistic technique to involve the reader in the sensibility of the speaker there is a novelistic satisfaction in here, even as those clearly observed and logically organized moments refuse to interlock as we might expect. The moments are novelistic, not the novel, and one result is a focus on details in which even an inanimate object can fill the foreground with hallucinatory force. A case in point is the narrator's wristwatch:

> Then I happened to look at my hand. And why wouldn't I? And how can I blame myself this time for yielding to spontaneity? Is there anything more logical for you to look, even without planning to, at your own hand, while waiting for whatever or whomever is coming?

The protestation of logic leads us to the watch itself.

> I had a watch on my wrist. Well who doesn't have one? I do admit though, it's not like other watches (I say honestly now, that is, during these moments in which I convey what happened, that I am not really sure this had any negative impact. At the same time I will also say, after a long consideration, that I am not at all sure it had a positive impact either. The presence of this watch on my wrist didn't change anything—I now believe—in the way the events unfolded, nor did it leave the slightest impression).

The narrator-author's unnerving denial of the watch's importance, after instructing the reader in the value of introspection and spontaneity, is funnier still when he does, in fact, describe it in detail. It is a Japanese watch, and in the way that possessors of expensive watches sometimes consider them indices of other values—magical links with a world of fashion or elegance—he seems to feel it defines him, that it even tells more about him than he wishes to be known.

> I breathed in deeply after reading them (the numbers) filling my lungs with air. I had a strange desire to suck in a lot of air, which was because I didn't find anything about the tiny writing on the edge of the watch that was cause for alarm. So why had I been afraid that the interrogators would be alarmed if they happened to see it, or find it suspicious, even if they were to assume the worst! (Is it wrong to call them interrogators?)

Is there something suspicious about the Japanese watch, or are these ruminations intended to cast further doubt on the narrator's fears? What do we make of the fact that the narrator, only a few lines earlier, tells us that he couldn't make out the tiny numbers with the naked eye and that he was only able to make them out eventually, once he got out alive? And did he eventually get out alive?

We come to learn a lot about this watch. It is a device to open wider the gap between the narrative and reader—even a source of comedy when the narrator discovers, to his surprise, that he has fumbled and fiddled with it, thinking so hard that he has inadvertently moved the hands, perhaps forward perhaps backward—who knows!—with the result that he can't even use his watch anymore for its main purpose—to tell time. The profound relation between punctuality and anxiety is a universal one, as the great Turkish satirist Ahmet Hamdi

Tanpinar makes visible in his novel *Saatleri Ayarlama Enstitüsü* (The Clock-Setting Institute), in which the hero sets out to synchronize all the clocks in Turkey, but Al-Daif makes that anxiety a metonymy for the fundamental split between subjective and objective experience. Meanwhile the watch is a deeper cause for anxiety because its numerals are—though it is a Japanese watch—in Arabic. And this reminds him of the many uncomfortable "interrogations" he suffered in the past from friends and acquaintances who were convinced that underlying his purchase of such a watch were subconscious Arab nationalist sentiments, perhaps even fanaticism. Like Gulliver's pocket watch, described by the Lilliputians in *Gulliver's Travels*, the narrator's wristwatch takes on a magnified, sinister, surreal materiality. And just as the narrator was asked in the previous watch-related episodes whether his real motivation behind buying the watch could not be attributed to "subconscious" sentiments of Arab fanaticism—how could he prove or disprove it?—in the interrogation room he eventually comes to the same conclusion concerning his innocence; for, even if he hadn't committed the crime for which he was under arrest, hadn't he wanted, deep down, to do such a thing? And such desires— weren't they cause for suspicion?

Readers of Robbe-Grillet's *The Voyeur* may feel that the narrator's introspection is more than a mood—it is a deliberate act of denial. Even the rare instances of dialogue serve only to comment on the narrator's doubts and anxieties. Indeed they cast doubt on his innocence and make us doubt the innocence of the title. (On which side of innocence are we located?) It is an appeal that sophisticated readers in the Arab world and in Europe have responded to, though al-Daif's writing has only begun to show up in the Anglophone world.

The first of al-Daif's novels to be translated into English was *Dear Mr. Kawabata* (*Azizi al-Sayyed Kawabata*, 1995—trans. Paul Starkey, Quartet Books, 1999; also translated into eight European languages), but he had already published eight novels in Arabic: the straightfaced, ironically titled *Unsi Yalhu Ma` Rita...* (Unsi Dallies with Rita, For Mature Readers, 1983), *Al-Mustabidd* (The Despot, 1983), *Fusha Mustahdafa Bayn al-Nu`as wa al-Nawm* (A Targeted Space Between Sleepiness and Sleep, 1986; in French, *Passage au Crepuscule*, 1992; English translation, 2000); *Ahl al-Zill* (People of the Shadow, 1987, translated into French as *Isolence du Serpent*), *Taqaniyyat al-Bu's* (The Techniques of Misery, 1989) and *Ghaflat al-Turab* (When the Soil Dozes Off, 1991). *Passage au Crépuscule* has already been made as a film in Switzerland. Following *Nahiyat al-Bara'a* (This Side of Innocence, 1997), al-Daif published two more novels: *Learning English* in 1999, and most recently *Tistifl Meryl Streep* (To Hell with Meryl Streep, January 2001).

When *This Side of Innocence* becomes a film we hope the screenwriter is not tempted to tell us too much about the characters, the motives, the narrator's innocence, or his childhood. Al-Daif has devised an esthetic system that values the unsaid and the unseen. It is an art of absences and negative shapes. We should learn to be satisfied with what he chooses to tell us about—things like the narrator's watch. For as this narrator tells us, even the "tiniest detail" might "trigger memory of the event." So al-Daif's tiny details take us gently, circuitously, but perhaps as swiftly as the mind can bear, into the heart of horror, in this examination of a human being and a country under unimaginable stress.

—Adnan Haydar & Michael Beard